We all took a little break after the *Panorama*, which you may remember, and went off to rest up and treat our papercuts and reintroduce ourselves to our loved ones, who had not seen us in some time. But after seven months as newspapermen and several weeks of blissful furlough, we came back hungry for a good old-fashioned short-story quarterly, the kind of issue we hadn't made since early last year, dense with well-nourished fiction—and that is what we set out to assemble. But then we were reminded of how good it is to include shorter pieces—including letters—among the longer stories we tend to run, so two pages beyond this one we've resurrected that practice, which we first took up way back in the first few issues of *McSweeney's*. And then, a couple hundred pages accounted for but still, somehow, hungry, we realized we were still a bit hooked on running long works of literary journalism, so here, in the other pocket of the plastic sleeve from which you retrieved this volume, we're proud to present Nick McDonell's stunning reporting from Iraq in a standalone paperback. Now, of course, the issue is just a hair under four hundred pages and we're feeling a bit wobbly on our feet, but we couldn't be happier with how it turned out, or with how we turned the damn thing around in two months. (Jan. 4–Mar. 4 being the working period for this issue—yes, we sent it to press on the calendar date that *corresponds to its issue number.* This will never happen again.) We had other ideas, too, involving untested inks and diagonal bands, but we're going to save those for another time. It's your continued support and enthusiasm that allows us to do that, to continue to do this, and so we thank you. INTERNS & VOLUNTEERS: Rennie Ament, Nicoletta Beyer, Hannah Edber, Laura Foxgrover, Adam Gray, Paul Keelan, Zac Stone, Becca Worby, Genevieve Walker, Michele Knapp, Meredith May, Kailyn McCord, Sarah Morrison, Jeffrey Mull, M. Rebekah Otto, Molly Prentiss, Stephen Reidy, Samantha Riley, Brady Welch, Gabrielle Zucker, Meagan Day. ALSO HELPING: Eli Horowitz, Andrew Leland, Greg Larson, Jesse Nathan. COPY EDITOR: Oriana Leckert. WEBSITE: Chris Monks. SUPPORT: Andi Mudd. OUTREACH: Juliet Litman. CIRCULATION: Adam Krefman. SENIOR EDITORS: Brian McMullen, Chris Ying, Michelle Quint. ASSOCIATE PUBLISHER: Laura Howard. MANAGING EDITOR: Jordan Bass. EDITOR: Dave Eggers.

COVER ILLUSTRATION: Self portrait by Siri Hustvedt. PREVIOUS PAGE: Will Eno. More self-portraits can be found on page 105.

Printed in Canada.

When McSweeney's *started out ten or so years ago, we regularly printed correspondence at the beginning of each journal. As an ode to that time, we're printing a letters section here, featuring some of the people from those original few issues, and some new ones, too.*

DEAR McSWEENEY'S,

I have recently become an expert on the subject of red wine.

Unfortunately, like many people, I was intimidated by red wine. It has so much complexity, history, and nuance that some people believe that it can only be enjoyed by scholars and wealthy narcissists.

But this is not true. For while red wine is noble, it is also humble. It is the simplest recipe in the world, requiring only grapes, yeast, human feet, and time, plus an enormous amount of pharmaceutical-grade pseudoephedrine. If you are going to make it at home, you should probably own a handgun and some really violent dogs.

This is how the European peasantry has made and enjoyed wine since 6000 BC. In quaint mobile wine labs, with thatched roofs, that still evade capture today.

In Europe, red wine remains a part of life. While we in the U.S. have long demonized alcohol, most Europeans are always drunk, and will frequently enjoy a glass of red wine even in the middle of one of their many naps.

In France, children do not hide their drinking. They join their parents at the dinner table, where they are served red wine, because it is believed it will make the children more sexy.

So how can you learn to enjoy red wine like the sexy French children?

It is easy.

Of all the varieties of wine—white wine, red wine, box wine, prison-toilet wine, and sparkling "Champagne," or "French Thunderbird"—the best kind of wine is red wine.

Named for its color, red wine has the most healthful tannins and antioxidants. This is why the baby boomers love it. For doctors agree, if you drink red wine, you will become immortal. You will start to look prosperous and self-pleased and salt-and-pepper-bearded, and you will learn to tell long, pointless stories that go nowhere because you love the sound of your own voice. To your health, rich dad!

Red wine also offers the greatest depth of flavor, ranging from the bright berry, ozone, and burnt hair notes of a jammy Cabernaz Beausoleil, to the luxuriously pungent Argentine velociraptors, with their end of bitter chocolate and chewed-up aluminum foil and fried crickets. These wines have the viscosity of marmite and spit, and connoisseurs know to not pour them, but to rub them on the bare chest like a poultice.

Some famous people who famously drank red wine include Val Kilmer.

Finally, a note on choosing a wine. You may think it's enough to just read Val Kilmer's red-wine blog and drink what he drinks. And for the most part, you'd do fine. But sometimes Val Kilmer gets confused and drinks Thousand Island dressing, and so it's important to develop your own taste, and your own palate.

Go to your reputable wine store and start exploring. Look at the labels. Does it have a kangaroo on it? That's probably a good wine.

Does it have a quirky picture of the winemaker's dog on it, and is it named for that crazy, funny, ugly dog? That's probably a good wine.

Make sure the font on the label is cool: no cursive, and easy on the serifs. And remember: no landscapes. If you buy a wine with a landscape on it, it means you are not intelligent.

And don't forget: some of the best red wine is synthesized right here in America. Try a tasting tour of the California's wine country, especially beautiful Lumlum and Subadadada counties. As you drink and drive and drink and drive from vineyard to vineyard, don't be afraid to ask questions.

Ask the salesperson: Is it a white wine? If it is, throw it on the ground. Is it red? Good, drink as much as you can, fast, and fall asleep in a field. Can the wine be colored red with blood? If so, then it is a rosé, and that is acceptable as well, especially if you are a Spaniard.

Thank you for your kind attention. To your health, rich dad!

That is all.

JOHN HODGMAN
BROOKLYN, NEW YORK

MR. McSWEENEY, OLD PAL—
Remember the opening credits of *Hawaii Five-O*, when Jack Lord stands on a roof surveying the panorama of then-mod Honolulu? I'm writing to you from a balcony—around here, they're called *lanai*—on the twentieth floor of the very same building, the Ilikai. It's one of the many concrete high-rises besmirching once-tranquil Waikiki, and was built in the post-'59 statehood architectural style I like to think of as A Very Brady Brutalism.

While I command the same view as Jack and his jawline, this morning it's yet another voggy day. Vog, the volcanic fog blowing over here from Kilauea, is the most exotic air pollution my landlubber's lungs have ever coughed up.

Last night I had to close the balcony's sliding doors and retreat inside to drown out the ukulele noise wafting from below. I don't know how many times I've come to these supposedly serene islands all the way from New York City only to be driven indoors by the racket of luaus or weddings or wedding luaus, which are the worst because of the deadly juncture of drums and drunks. I didn't come here for the umbrella drinks. I chose to stay in this building because it's walking distance to the Mission Houses Museum library and archives, a treasure-trove of letters and journals left by the churchy New Englanders who arrived here in 1820 to Christianize the local heathen.

To give you an idea of what they were like, yesterday I read a letter written by Abner Wilcox, a missionary on the neighboring island of Kauai, which he sent to his sons in 1861 while they were studying at Yale. The Civil War had just started, and Wilcox opined that the Union army had endured "panic and defeat" at the Battle of Bull Run because it had "desecrated the Sabbath." (Bull Run having been the skirmish in which the stubborn Stone-wall Jackson got his famous nickname is apparently trumped by blatant commandment-breaking on a Sunday.) In the same collection of Wilcox's papers I also found a memo he received in 1838 from his sponsors, the American Board of Commissioners for Foreign Missions. It asked their missionaries scattered around the globe to send back to Boston items for a cabinet of curiosities they were assembling at headquarters, including "warlike weapons," because "these convey a vivid idea of the savageness of heathenism, and impress the beholder with the reality of the dark places of the earth, which are full of the habitations of cruelty."

Speaking of the habitations of cruelty, did you know that the Ilikai was designed by one of the architects of Seattle's Space Needle? Or that it was the very first luxury high-rise hotel in the state? And that Elvis used to stay here? Or that its developer, Chinn Ho, was a self-made millionaire who rose from peddling can openers to become the first Asian to run the Honolulu

Stock Exchange? Or that Detective Chin Ho Kelly on *Hawaii Five-0* was named after him? Which is a nice change of pace, since most things around here are named for long-dead Hawaiian monarchs. Like, I wonder if Chin Ho Kelly or even Chinn Ho himself ever got their cavities filled at the King Kalakaua Dental Center.

Wish you were here!

SARAH VOWELL
HONOLULU, HAWAII

DEAR McSWEENEY'S,

You know when you're at an awkward Q&A after a reading or something, and somebody stands up and says, "I have more of a comment than a question"? Because I love that.

JULIE KLAUSNER
NEW YORK CITY

DEAR MUM,

They'll love you in LA, I just know it. The City of Angels will finally have a genuine piece of the divine. You will get an agent, and a trainer, and a bunch of lawyers and a business manager and a publicist. You will get a personal assistant and bodyguards and a personal stylist. You will have an accountant and a yoga coach and a number of charities you support. You will be a celebrity.

You will go on the Oprah show and talk about how great it is to hit the limelight after fifty, and you and Oprah and the one billion or so women watching will have half a dozen *Aha!* moments, and then you'll sing. You will teach Martha Stewart how to cook an African dish on national TV—but please, Mum, keep it simple. Fry dodo, or if you must cook soup, let it be *egusi*. Oh, and small balls of *eba* for the swallowing, Mum, small balls for the swallowing.

You will move into a big house with a pool and a history. You will remodel the house and reinvent yourself. In spite of your strongest urges, you will become a vegan. You will finally lose the weight you gained from bearing three strong sons, and from gathering for yourself the largest chunks of meat and fat from every dish you cooked. You will live on the treadmill until you are thin enough to jog on the beach with your trainer and your bodyguards and the paparazzi.

You will get a famous yogi-to-the-stars and dabble actively in Pilates. You will do your best to get your body in its best shape, Mum, and then you will use other procedures to add and subtract as you see fit. But all things in moderation. Do not forget Kanye's mother, and our very own Stella. I trust you will exercise your judgment, as you always have. And don't worry: there are surgeons who can be counted on to do a good job on the down-low, very hush-hush. They say discretion is the better part of LA.

Even though you are an LA-based celebrity, you will not forget Nigeria, Mum. You will speak of the country of your birth with nostalgia, but not too much. Measured wistfulness, Mum. You will romanticize your childhood: the ten-mile, barefoot journey to school, your struggling mother, your days in the village choir—especially Sunday services, when you would unfailingly bring the entire congregation of quasi-heathens to tears with your gospel solos. Mention as often as you can how grateful you are to be in the Land of the Free. Stay away from those Naija people in Houston. They are bad news. Speak favorably of Nigeria, but do nothing to shatter Western myths of impoverished sub-Saharan Africa: the junkyard of pity and aid. The bastion of famine, and conflict, and AIDS.

You, Mum, will be the continent's brightest export, brighter even than blood diamonds.

You will take a leaf from hip-hop. You will "have a beef" with an established and successful female singer, preferably black. I would suggest Whitney Houston, but it would be a waste of time. Actually, forget all the African American singers. Forget Diana, forget Patti, never mind Mary J., and don't even think an uncomplimentary thought about Tina or Beyoncé. Jay-Z has been known to stab people.

Call out Sade (for her irritating sultriness), or Kidjo (for her suspicious mannishness, and also for that nasty haircut)—in short, whoever has an album that's showing up on the charts. If you go to France, be sure to say something really mean about Asa. If you are in London, try and record a song with Amy Winehouse, but make sure Mark Ronson produces it, and keep a bodyguard and a can of pepper spray close; that girl can be a handful. Then, when you are safely back across the pond, tell a magazine or E! news how horrible it was working with Amy.

Beef can do wonders for careers. Just go to Lagos and ask Ruggedman, if he's not in London performing. Don't listen to that crazy Afeni Shakur and Marsha Wallace telling sob stories they've been telling for many, many decades. Since the '90s.

Then there will be Vegas and Broadway. I can see it now: you will be asked to have your own reality show. We'll have giraffes and zebras on the lawn, and there'll be constant bickering among us, your sons. Who knows, you may be seeing a nice gentleman at the time, and maybe we'll let him appear on the show as well. Whatever you do in LA, Mum, don't act like Mariah Carey and have a marriage that will be an embarrassment to your boys. Don't carry on like Hulk Hogan's wife or Ivana Tramp.

We'll be instant stars, all of us. But first you'll have to get the network to talk U.S. Immigration into forgiving my past deportations and letting me back into the country. I look forward to my first authentic U.S. visa.

I will tell you more later, Mum. But you better believe it. Your time, *our* time, has come. I guess all that tithing and praying and fasting has finally paid off. I hope you renewed your passport as I told you to months ago. I swear on my mother's life, Mum. They'll absolutely love you in LA.

SODIENYE KURUBO
PORT HARCOURT, NIGERIA

DEAR McSWEENEY'S,

You know what else I love at a Q&A is when the person who stands up to ask a question is way more interested in showing the room how they know certain things or important people (basically nouns), than they are in getting their question answered.

Because one time I was splitting a turkey wrap with Mackenzie Phillips at this café (Mack's an old friend—she's such a lamb, only with a shocking incest history), and she told me about how, in France, they won't serve you a cappuccino after breakfast. I know what you're thinking! "Why not?" Because they are assholes.

JULIE KLAUSNER
NEW YORK CITY

DEAR SIRS AND MADAMS,

There are cities whose geography condemns their meteorologists to report bad news from time to time: a hurricane, an earthquake, a flood. Lima has condemned its own to announce the same sad forecast every day for nine months: cloudy skies with no rain. This grayness—the shade of cement, elephants, smoke, pipes, and some coins—is the color of waiting. In Lima we live waiting for summer, for umbrellas that do not exist. Springtime is a lie that appears in schoolbooks. The sky shifts between albino and ash, and between these extremes lies an invitation to stare at our feet. In *Remarks on Color*, Ludwig Wittgenstein says "There is no such thing as luminous gray. Is that part of the concept of gray, or part of the psychology, i.e., of the natural history of gray?" The German philosopher never visited this city, and so failed to realize his error: the sky of Lima is a luminous gray, a tone with which its inhabitants try to coexist while the sun struggles to penetrate the thick curtain of clouds, calling it "the sky of a donkey's belly" in lighthearted resignation. Though the Eskimos have distinguished more than thirty types of snow, no one has broken down the myriad grays that a single sky can hold. An as-yet-unwritten history of the apocalyptic sky would have to be the work of someone born in Lima.

The fog of London competes with the sky of Lima. In the nineteenth century, unable to free himself from the memory of having been here, Herman Melville wrote one of the most beautiful literary curses ever earned by any place on earth: "tearless Lima, the strangest, saddest city thou can'st see." Has a blue sky ever moved a writer like the moribund sky of this city? In *Moby-Dick*, Melville added: "For Lima has taken the white veil; and there is a higher horror in this whiteness of her woe." It is both scientific and poetic to say that Lima's sky depresses: serotonin, the hormone produced by the brain in direct proportion to the amount of natural light that the human body receives, helps to restore a person's mood. The people of Lima tend toward melancholy. At night, the heavenly landscape refuses contemplation by poets and astronomers. When Allen Ginsberg passed through Lima, he could not resist mentioning that crushing donkey's belly above him: "To be a poet's a serious occupation, condemned to that in universe—to walk the city ascribbling in a book—just accosted by a drunk in Plaza de Armas sidestreet under a foggy sky, and sometimes with no moon," he writes in *Reality Sandwiches*.

Ginsberg exaggerated: by night in Lima, the stars are indeed barely visible, but not even our sky is so bashful as to hide the moon. Founded upon a desert, between the Pacific Ocean and the barren Andean mountains, Lima breathes restlessly within an atmospheric prison of clouds and smog. Its gray is of astronomical proportions, and has inoculated its residents against temperamental excess, with the exception of their devotion to their own cuisine. While the *Dictionary of the Royal Spanish Academy*, ignoring Lima, defines the sky first and foremost as an "apparently blue and diaphanous sphere that surrounds the Earth," perhaps it is Robert Walser who manages a more just description of Lima and the effects of its sky. In his novel *The Walk*, a poet steps out of his house and finds himself suddenly before a woman whom he takes to be Peruvian. "She had a certain pale and faded majesty," says the Swiss writer, who ended his days in a madhouse.

JULIO VILLANUEVA CHANG
FOUNDING EDITOR,
ETIQUETA NEGRA MAGAZINE
LIMA, PERU
translated by Daagya Dick

DEAR McSWEENEY'S,

I'd like to tell you about the time my great uncle Owen came over for Thanksgiving. We were all very excited to have him join us, because he was a famous actor. Well, perhaps "famous" is an exaggeration. He'd played a villain who got shot by Robert Redford in *Butch Cassidy and the Sundance Kid*, and later on he appeared as a large dancing rabbit in one of the Muppet movies. He'd also done some work on Broadway, but he never revealed just what that was.

Anyway, it was my job was to pick him up at the airport. I was sixteen years old, and had just recently gotten my driver's license. I felt grateful for the responsibility. In fact, I was assigned to be Uncle Owen's driver for the entire weekend, because he didn't drive.

"A true thespian does not require a vehicle," he told me.

Uncle Owen had long, flowing gray hair, which he parted to the side. He looked a bit like a Confederate general. Whenever he met someone, he would say, "I'm most pleased to make your acquaintance." And then he would bow. It was very charming.

"At what time shall we be dining in the morrow?" Uncle Owen asked my mother, when we got home.

"Four o'clock," she told him.

"Splendid," said Uncle Owen.

Uncle Owen pointed to his suitcase and had me bring it upstairs. He would be sleeping in my room while I slept downstairs on the couch.

"Thank you for your kind assistance, my good man," he said to me.

"Good night, Uncle Owen," I said.

Each year my mother would concoct this special turkey brine in which she would soak the bird overnight. It was a secret mixture of salt water, butter, tomato paste, olive oil, and several unknown spices. She took a lot of care and pride in making it. Guests from far and wide had commented on the deliciousness of my mother's turkey recipe.

That night, as I slept on the couch downstairs, I heard a strange thumping sound coming from the kitchen. I went in there to investigate it, and what should I discover but old Uncle Owen, bare naked in the pale moonlight, humping our raw turkey with all his might. The two nubby drumsticks were poking out awkwardly from around his waist, and the slippery bird carcass was flopping back and forth across the counter with each vivacious thrust. Uncle Owen was in surprisingly good shape for an old man. He remained so absorbed in this activity that he didn't even notice me standing there.

"Uncle Owen," I finally said.

"Whoa!" he shouted, jumping back and tossing the bird quickly away from him. It smacked against the wall and slid to the floor in a heap.

"My good man," said Uncle Owen, catching his breath, "you nearly started me to death!"

We both stood there gazing at the limp, raw turkey laying on the floor.

"What were you doing to our turkey?" I asked.

"I was merely tenderizing it," he said. He was covered practically head-to-toe in my mother's secret brining sauce.

"Maybe you should take a shower," I suggested.

Uncle Owen surveyed the mess in the kitchen. The counter was soaked in sauce, and a greasy splotch marked the spot on the wall where the turkey carcass had struck when he had tossed it away.

"Yes, well, I do believe a hot bath might be in order."

And with that Uncle Owen left the kitchen, still naked and glistening with sauce. I set about cleaning up the place. I was unsure how to replace the secret brining mixture, since the recipe had yet to be passed down to my generation. I approximated things as best I could, though, wiped the place dry, and got back to bed around dawn.

That afternoon we all gathered around the table and said grace, heads bowed. My mother concluded by saying, "We are particularly grateful for the presence of our dear Uncle Owen..."

And we all said, "Amen."

The big turkey was carved, and my mother took the first bite. She said, "There's something quite different about this bird..."

We were all quiet. My mother took another bite, savoring the mouthful thoughtfully. "Yes, this is a most peculiar flavor... and it's the best turkey I've ever tasted!"

Someone shouted, "Hip, hip hooray!" and we all cheered together. Now, I don't know if it was Uncle Owen's special tenderizing method, or maybe it was my particular alteration of that secret soaking sauce, but we all did agree that it was the very best Thanksgiving turkey we had ever eaten.

Uncle Owen never did return for another Thanksgiving with us, but he did appear briefly in the motion picture *Little Man Tate* alongside the famous actress Jodie Foster. He played a psychiatrist. And I received a postcard from him some time after that. It said:

Although we are not romantically involved, I have impregnated Ms. Foster, the actress.

In 1991, Jodie Foster received an Academy Award for her work in the film *The Silence of the Lambs*. Her acceptance speech was succinct and to the point, but we were all much surprised and delighted when, at the very end, she chose to dedicate her award to "My dear friend Owen, for everything he has done."

ARTHUR BRADFORD
PORTLAND, OREGON

DEAR EDITOR,

The most racially diverse place I've ever seen is the playground in Tirso de Molina Square, just two blocks from my house. Over there, the immigrant children of the neighborhood—Bangladeshis and Senegalese and Ecuadorians—all romp and roughhouse together, yelling at each other in perfect Spanish slang. The children are like an army out of *Lord of the Flies*; if they have parents, I've never seen them. Their absent guardians may be any of the neighborhood's small-business owners, whose eclectic shops purvey phone cards, Bollywood movies, melons, and milk.

I am writing to you from Lavapiés, in central Madrid: the stomping ground of transvestites, immigrants, artists, and widows. Mostly, though, it is a neighborhood of phone shops. Here in Spain they're called *locutorios*, which an old friend of mine translates as "talkatorium." For better or worse, Lavapiés is almost universally associated with phone shops, the immigrant small business *par excellence*. One of these phone shops was owned by the Moroccans who planned and executed the March 2004 train bombings in Madrid. The owners have changed, but the store still stands in Plaza

Lavapiés, boasting advertisements for discount phone cards to Africa, Asia, and Latin America. My favorite card is CHILLI TALK; its poster, with a woman seductively holding a pepper between her lips, suggests a direct relationship between international calls and phone sex.

If the playground in Tirso de Molina Square is a postcard for post-Franco Spain's triumphant multiculturalism, Lavapiés's other squares tell a less optimistic story. Every other square seems to have a nationality or ethnic group associated with it, creating a succession of recreational ghettos. Many immigrants live in crowded apartments, with as many as eight people to a bedroom; since their domestic space provides no respite, and they can't afford to hang out in Lavapiés's numerous bars and cafés, they tend to congregate in open public spaces. Madrileños complain that the immigrants have "taken over" the city's plazas.

Down the street from my apartment, at the intersection of Calle Lavapiés and Calle de los Ministriles Chica, there's a small square where the sizeable Senegambian population congregates. Spain has no open-container laws, so the environment resembles something of an outdoor party—'80s-style boom boxes and bottles of beer. The city police regularly come by to pester the Senegambians for loitering. The other day, as I walked by, I struck up a conversation with Derrick, a young Gambian man whom I see there most days. He was wearing a Tupac T-shirt with the sleeves rolled up. Derrick told me that he had been in Spain for two years, but that he was out of work now. I asked him why some people referred to his country as Gambia and others as The Gambia, but he seemed confused by my question. Afterward I was embarrassed by my twee curiosity: I'm sure that an unemployed African man in Spain has bigger fish to fry than the article (or lack thereof) attached to his country's name.

Lavapiés is filled with contradictions. If you go down Calle Lavapiés toward the eponymous square, you'll find Bar el Jamón (Ham Bar). Right next to it, there are three halal butchers. Like Bar el Jamón, the street names in the area seem to belong to a Spain of a different era: Ave María, Calvario, San Carlos, Jesús y María. The colorful storefronts, however, paint a more accurate picture of the neighborhood's latest demographics. Casa de Bangladesh, a store that abuts the Senegambians' meeting square, advertises its goods as "Food, Clothes, and Fashion of India, Chinese, Arabic, and Spain." The storefront of Asia Travels & Money Transfer Spain is an even better snapshot of the neighborhood's commerce: phone cards, a Western Union advertisement for remittances, and travel deals to Tangier, Quito, and Delhi. The store is owned by Moroccans and operated by a polyglot Bangladeshi man. This mix makes it the closest adult analogue I've found of the multicultural playground in Tirso de Molina Square.

During our first week in the neighborhood, my fiancée went to Asia Travels & Money Transfer Spain to make some copies. We had just moved from Morocco to Madrid, and her Spanish was still shaky. She ended up speaking with the Bangladeshi clerk in Moroccan Arabic, to the astonishment of the largely South Asian clientele and the Moroccan owners. I think her encounter may suggests the best definition of Lavapiés: a neighborhood where the shortest line between a Bangladeshi man and a six-foot-tall blond American woman is Moroccan Arabic.

ERIC CALDERWOOD
MADRID, SPAIN

DEAR MCSWEENEY'S,

Basically, I go to a lot of things that have Q&As at the end of them, okay? Not you asked and that this is a Q&Q. Laughing out loud!

Anyway, so the last thing I love about Q&As is when somebody stands up and asks a question, and then the moderator or the person in the front of the room or whatever repeats the question into the microphone they have access to so that everybody else in the room can hear. Like "The question was, 'Where do you get your ideas.'" And they say it like a statement and not a question? Even though I said that like a question and it was more of a statement.

Because if they don't repeat what somebody said into a microphone, somebody old—and there's *always* somebody old at a Q&A, it's like the "A" stands for Elderly, or Alderly, which I think I read once was Alan Alda's name before they changed it on Allis Island—will be like "Speak up!," and they mean "Speak up, sonny!" but they don't say "sonny" anymore because of racism. Also, old people used to carry ear trumpets around with them for that very reason (racism), but now, an ear trumpet is something that reads like an affected prop, like when teenagers buy glasses with clear frames or take up smoking a pipe. Not that kind of pipe! Not all teenagers are like your teenager.

Okay, we have time for one more question. We don't? Okay then, never mind.

JULIE KLAUSNER
NEW YORK CITY

DEAR McSWEENEY'S,

I've never tried to explain why I keep coming back here. It could be that in some ways I don't grasp it myself. I just get on the plane again and off the plane again and then I'm here.

I didn't plan this trip. It was an impulse. I had work to do but that wasn't it. It hit me that it was Ramadan and I've never been here during Ramadan. Something unexpected always happens. I might come a hair closer—the answer to one more of my questions about Cairo might reveal itself when I least expect it to. But also, after all the messiness of the past year, it was something of a gift to myself. Every Ramadan I spent in Morocco felt somehow cleansing. I actually like fasting, the strictness of nothing passing between your lips, not food, not water, not a cigarette, not even gum or a toothbrush or a kiss. The intensity of it.

The night I arrived, I got to the hotel just before 1 a.m. I keep a cell phone for Egypt, with an Egyptian SIM card and my Cairo phone number in it, and it runs out of batteries between trips—it uses a Euro plug (two prongs), and the network doesn't work in Chicago, so I can't check it when I'm away from here. But when I turn it on, it's like magic—it reconnects me to this world in a way that Facebook never can. By 2 a.m. I was out with a friend.

We ended up at his place, talking and drinking the last of the Scotch that his British girlfriend had brought him, and then it was almost 4 a.m. and I was teasing him about something when the call to prayer started. I had no idea dawn would come so early. It was still pitch dark outside—it turns out that they moved up daylight savings time by about six weeks to make Ramadan work a bit better for everyone. And his girlfriend says "You better hurry" so he runs to the refrigerator to gulp down a half liter of water before he can't drink for the rest of the day. When he rejoins us he says, "The call to prayer is like a pyramid, and I caught it before the peak, so it's okay." Sunset these days is at 6:30 p.m., and it's 97 degrees outside when the sun's out, so drinking that water will come in handy. But even so he sleeps most of the day. No job. Well, he's a writer.

The days have a special rhythm here in Ramadan. People stay up so late, maybe because of the abundant Iftar meals at sunset that stretch out like a month of Thanksgivings. Sometimes there's a lighter meal before dawn (*sohour*), and then you snooze away the daylight till it starts up again. You're wondering how people with regular jobs can do this. But I have another friend here who works in an office, and he met us downtown for sohour tonight on this boat on the Nile. There was *ta'amiyya* (falafel) and tamarind juice and live music, and the call to prayer started just as we climbed into taxis.

I've fasted before, but this time I have too much work to do to struggle through the day without some nourishment, so I modified the law. I'm doing a coffee fast: no food, no water, just coffee when the sun is up. To be honest, it's not so hard. I can't eat for the first few hours after I wake anyway, and then you're almost there, so why not push all the way through? And it's putting me into this state where just as I get to that time of the day when my writing comes best, I'm half hallucinating from the caffeine and the dehydration and it's something between automatic writing and writing drunk. I love it. And when I go out rushing to meet whomever for Iftar I'm eager and wired and that first taste of food is so perfect. You really should fast, if ever you get a chance.

It's 5 a.m. now, and the sun is coming up. I'm not sure if it's just easier to stay on Chicago time, since going to bed at dawn here is like going to bed when you'd go to bed there. Night here starts when an imam somewhere in the Saudi desert can't distinguish between a black thread and a white thread. Morning begins when the first thread of sunlight scratches the eastern sky. Those are the hinges upon which Ramadan turns.

But I have to tell you about something I saw yesterday that I hadn't noticed before. I was passing under this bridge that crosses over the Nile and then lets out in Zamalek, where I'm staying. There were rows of empty tables beneath it; I had made my way between them earlier in the day without thinking about it. But when I came back, at about 6, they were filled with people sitting quietly—waiting. Someone told me they're called *ma'idat er-rahman*—tables of mercy. They're for poor people who can't afford to cook a big Iftar, or for people who can't get back to their homes in time to break the fast, and they're paid for by rich people or mosques or neighborhood associations. Zamalek is a wealthy neighborhood by Cairo standards, and I don't know if that's why, but the food they brought out looked good—meat and soup and baby zucchinis stuffed with more meat and green peppers. And so I waited there just watching without seeming to watch while the people waited for the call to prayer to permit them to start. One man, dark like a Nubian from the south, had his head down on the table, maybe tired, maybe dehydrated. There was a hush of anticipation, a sense of community, of shared purpose. I'm not a religious person, but at moments like that I miss a connection to something bigger, to something infinite.

Cairo has 16 million people living in it. At times, when you walk up the busiest thoroughfares, you can feel like a speck, just a granule of dirt in this city where pollution smothers the sky and smears the walls right down to the pavement. It could be I want to be forgotten, to disappear into the 16 million Cairenes making their way through a city that will forget them, never knew them, breathes them with filthy lungs coated with centuries of grime and anonymity. But then at those tables of mercy there was a moment—it took me aback—of peace and silence and anticipation. It happens each day, after depriving yourself—and I was depriving myself, too, in my way, I was coffee fasting—that brief and gorgeous moment of cool water coming down your throat and into your belly. You have passed another day of glory on this earth and in this city that has been here since the time of Khufu.

BRIAN T. EDWARDS
CAIRO, EGYPT

DEAR EDITORS,

Did you guys see how bestselling seventeen-year-old German novelist Helene Hegemann has been accused of plagiarism after it was revealed that her debut novel, *Axolotl Roadkill*, contains passages lifted from a blog about sex and drugs in Berlin's techno scene? Although she's agreed to include acknowledgment of her source material in the next edition of the book, she denies she did anything wrong: "I can't understand what all the fuss is about."

I couldn't agree more. As you've heard me say a million times, *Axolotl* and like-minded writers' books are awash in conscious, self-conscious, conspicuous appropriation because they want to regain the freedoms that writers from Montaigne to Burroughs took for granted but that we have lost. To take one among innumerable examples, two-thirds of Shakespeare's *Henry VI* is taken directly from other sources, none of which, of course, are cited.

The "plagiarized" sections of Hegemann's book were written by a blogger calling himself Airen, who took any drugs he could get his hands on, including ecstasy, speed, cocaine, heroin, and ketamine, and had sex with anyone, including men, women, and transvestites, in clubs like Berghain, in toilets, anywhere—all so he could blog about it. In *The Arcades Project*, Walter Benjamin writes, "Method of this project: literary montage. I needn't say anything. Merely show. I shall purloin no valuables, appropriate no ingenious formulations. But the rags, the refuse—these I will not inventory but allow, in the only way possible, to come into their own: by making use of them." I practically have these lines tattooed to my forehead. Or as Josh Billings, Twain's contemporary, said, "About the most originality that any writer can hope to achieve honestly is to steal with good judgment."

Airen chronicled his hedonist experiences in a book called *Strobo*, a reworking of his blog posts. A few hundred copies of the book sold, one apparently to Helene Hegemann. Analogy: in Michael Lesy's *Wisconsin Death Trip*, the art consists of taking someone else's material and reframing it. Lesy juxtaposes photographs taken by Charles van Schaik with historical documents from turn-of-the-century Jackson County, Wisconsin, to create what he calls "an experiment in both history and alchemy"—the alchemy being Lesy's transformation of American pastoral into Edvard Munch nightmare. Hegemann provided Airen with noir context: a generation of German youth set in a bohemian attitude manual. He seems not to understand.

"*Axolotl* is full of interesting sections," Airen says. "There was really no need for her to copy me. But she borrowed entire passages of dialogue. I feel like my copyright has been infringed." Art, though, is a conversation between and among artists; it's not a patent office. Reality can't be copyrighted. See the recent movie *The Last Station*, much of which is focused on Tolstoy's attempt to give to the Russian people copyright to his works. "Berlin is here to mix everything with everything," one of Hegemann's characters says, in English. "I help myself wherever I find inspiration and ideas: films, music, books, paintings, poetry about sausages, photos, conversations, dreams… precisely because my work and my theft become authentic the moment something touches my soul. Who cares where I get things from? All that matters is what I do with them." "So it's not by you, then?" someone asks him. "No. It's by some blogger."

"I am quite content to go down to posterity as a scissors-and-paste man," James Joyce wrote seventy years ago. Love that quote; love it to death. William Gibson says, "Who owns the words? Who owns the music and the rest of our culture? We do. All of us. Though not all of us know it, yet." Art, not to mention life, now seems to happen primarily in liminal spaces, edited, quoted and quoted again and recontextualized, re-placed, collaged, stitched together. The mimetic function has been replaced by manipulation of the original (surely you agree?).

DAVID SHIELDS
SEATTLE, WASHINGTON

DEAR MCSWEENEY'S,

I have long been meaning to bring this to your attention, but: As fine as your magazine is—and it is quite fine—there nevertheless seems to be something lacking: a mascot. All the great magazines have mascots. *Playboy*, of course, has its bowtie-wearing bunny—or "Geoffrey, the Fancy Rabbit," as I have named him. (I actually have developed a backstory for the *Playboy* bunny, available upon request.) The *New Yorker* has Eustace Tilley, the near-sighted lepidopterist, forever examining a butterfly atop the magazine's masthead. And *Ranger Rick* has Ranger Rick, the friendly raccoon. (Side note: Did you know that raccoons are actually nocturnal animals, and, if you see one in daylight, there's a decent chance that it has rabies? This bit of information sheds a whole new light on Ranger Rick, doesn't it? He's actually kind of a tragic figure, struggling just to get through the day and share his love of nature, all the while trying desperately not to think about how much he wants to bite someone's face off. He's like Edward from *Twilight*, but with a greater propensity toward marking his territory with glandular secretions.)

Those are just three examples of great magazines that have mascots. There are many, many others. *Mad* magazine, for instance. That's four.

So: Where's your mascot? Lovely

though your illustrations are, none of them cries out and says, "Yes! I am the embodiment of *McSweeney's*!" I have taken the liberty of coming up with a few possibilites for you. (Unfortunately, my drawing abilities are limited, but I can see each of them quite clearly in my head, and would be willing to work with a graphic artist to help realize my visions. Rest assured: I am not afraid to say "No, that's not it, try again!" as many times as it takes until the drawing resembles exactly what I imagine.)

- Jim, the *McSweeney's* bird (he's wearing a cardigan sweater and he's got an air of erudition about him—he's lighting a pipe and doing that thing that practiced pipe-smokers do, where they tilt their heads to one side and squint one eye as they light it, in order to keep the smoke out; obviously, there will be a disclaimer at the bottom, warning kids against the dangers of smoking)

- Doug, the *McSweeney's* goat (he's standing on his hind legs, wearing overalls, winking and giving a thumbs-up, as if to say, "That's right, you know what I'm talking about!")

- Harry Dean Stanton, the *McSweeney's* Harry Dean Stanton (it's just Harry Dean Stanton, waving hello)

Those are just three suggestions—I have many more. Just let me know if you're interested, and I will get to work. Sincerely,

TIM CARVELL
NEW YORK CITY

DEAR McSWEENEY'S,

I'm still waiting to hear from you on my mascot idea, but I figured I'd pass along just a small taste of my unpublished novel about the *Playboy* bunny:

The Playboy *Bunny, or:*
Geoffrey, the Fancy Rabbit

Geoffrey put on his bowtie, adjusted it carefully, and looked in the mirror. He knew the other rabbits were laughing at him for his affectations—the bowtie, the jodhpurs, the habit of referring to drugstores as "chemists" and trucks as "lorries," the habit of spelling his name "Geoffrey" instead of "Jeffrey." But he didn't care. He simply felt that a rabbit wasn't fully dressed unless he was wearing some sort of evening wear. Did that make him

> pretentious? Very well, then. He was pretentious. But better to be pretentious than to be plain, to be common, to be just another goddamn rabbit.

There's more where that came from! Seriously. There's, like, five hundred pages more. I await your reply.

Sincerely,

TIM CARVELL
NEW YORK CITY

DEAR MCSWEENEY'S,

I am slowly going blind from an eye condition called Retinitis Pigmentosa. It's strange to think that among the things I'll miss most once I'm without vision won't be the sight of ocean sunsets, for example, reflected off of my (hypothetical) daughters' smile-framed teeth, but instead the way that printed semicolons look as they hover next to my favorite clauses from comic British novels published in the 1980s.

ANDREW LELAND
SAN FRANCISCO, CALIFORNIA

DEAR MCSWEENEY'S,

I was recently fired from a writing job which consisted of reviewing complimentary baby products sent to us in the mail. After being fired I learned that the unwritten contract between baby-product companies and such writers states that we're supposed to give everything a good review in return for getting it free. What a load of crap! I include here a couple reviews, which perhaps you'll print in the name of freedom:

BABESTA.COM
DUCK BOTTLE HUGGER

This was one of those products we got in the mail and thought, "Now what the hell is this thing?" We really couldn't figure it out for a while, because we got it without the packaging, which explained that it was a "bottle hugger." The idea is that it helps your baby hold the bottle while keeping the bottle cold (or warm) as well. It also protects the bottle from breaking when your kid flings it across the room. Of course, such a function could be accomplished just as easily without the stuffed-duck apparatus, but then it wouldn't be so cute and theoretically appealing to your child. Our daughter was not a huge fan of the Duck Bottle Hugger, but she's still a little young for such things. We gave it to another set of parents who have an older son (pretending we'd bought it for them as a gift, of course), and they said that their son really liked it. It wasn't that convincing a claim, though, and when we revealed that it wasn't actually a gift, they revealed that they actually rarely used it. In fact, the father said, the best use he'd found for it was as a funny way to hold his beer. Isn't this the way it is with most of these damn baby products? I bet some kids really like their duck bottle huggers, but I also bet you could survive quite well without it. My wife suggested that sex-deprived new fathers might employ the soft duck mouth as a masturbation aid, and I must admit this seemed like a very fine idea to me. Just don't get caught.

Starfish Bathtub Thermometer

This cute starfish-shaped piece of plastic performs not one, but two functions. 1) As you fill the bath, you stick the starfish to the wall of your tub at the desired water level, and when it reaches that height a shrill alarm goes off, thus saving you from overfilling the tub and spilling water all over the floor. 2) It has a thermometer which tells you the exact temperature of the water, so you don't burn your baby's sensitive skin. I'll address function number 1 first: the suction cup, like most suction cups I've encountered in bathtub/shower situations, is unreliable. The starfish kept falling into the water, and then the alarm would go off too soon. Plus the alarm isn't even that loud, so if you're far away you likely won't hear it over the filling water. Function number 2: The thermometer works fine, but really, can't we just feel the water and know when it's too hot for our baby? To be honest, I don't even know what the proper temperature is, numberwise, but I do know when things are too hot. My wife disagrees with me on this point, though, and she often thinks I'm going to do something careless and maim our child, so I do think it was helpful for her to actually see scientific proof that the bathwater was of suitable temperature. So, in conclusion, here's another one of those products which you could no doubt live without owning, but maybe you'd find it useful if you got it as a gift, or, say, if the website you write for sent it to you for free as a product review. But really, when do us new parents get to draw the line on all these semi-useful plastic pieces of crap filling up our homes? I'd say draw it somewhere before you buy one of these things. It's time for a revolution, people! But first I'm going to take a goddamn bath.

ARTHUR BRADFORD
PORTLAND, OREGON

LIKE THE LOCKED ANTLERS

by LAWRENCE-MINH BÙI DAVIS

Không trông mông giúp thì sẽ không thất-vọng
—Painted on a rooftop in Village de L'est, Ninth Ward, New Orleans.
Roughly translated: *Don't expect help, you won't be disappointed*

THERE ARE THREE kinds of reporters: the ones who work at a big paper and know they're hot shit; the ones who work at a little paper and think they're hot shit; and the ones who work at a paper where the editor-in-chief, advice columnist, and janitor are all a guy named Hung.

This is the breakdown on the current junket, at least. I'm in the third category. It's November 2005 and I'm on assignment, reporting on the aftermath of Hurricane Katrina for the *Vietnamese American Gazette*. I'm traveling with the big fish—a couple of reporters from the Orange County papers, one each from the Viet Am papers in Houston, Northern Virginia, and the Bay Area, and a Viet One Channel TV correspondent. We even have a helicopter, or rather the gentleman from the Viet One Channel has one, and he's kindly let the rest of us tag along.

Not one of us—probably not one member of the Viet diaspora anywhere—misses the connection between this disaster and the exodus of the boat people. That's why we're here, really, why this is *news* news. Water to water, tragedy to tragedy, and again, in death, find life.

To say the devastation is indescribable is to accept the age-old maxim about the incommensurability of language and experience. It's the path taken by a good many reporters and the majority of emergency responders and politicians. *Too much to take in. Incomprehensible. Beggars description.* It's also the easy way out.

Our helicopter is a Bell 206L3 LongRanger, sleek black with massive horsepower and state-of-the-art FLIR video equipment. My colleagues are Mr. Bảo, fifty-four, heavyset, raspy, and cranky; Mr. Đê, sixty-six, lanky and dressed like a dandy; Mr. Giang, forty-nine, elegant, smooth, and not-so-secretly a very angry person; and three other guys whose names I haven't gotten yet. I'm the only woman in the group. My name is Karen Nguyễn. Smoker, no kids, not married, considerably younger than the rest.

According to our pilot, the black water once stretched as far as the eye can see, but after a few days it's drained, leaving pretty much what we see now: abandoned cars, toppled trees, not a single unbroken building. Ahead on the left is a destroyed townhouse complex; on the right, a wrecked elementary school. Behind the school is a field of shanties made of tarpaulins held up by what look to be repurposed soccer goals and uprooted signposts. Maybe the devastation *is* indescribable.

After an hour we touch down on a helipad on the north side of the city. The others are clamoring over what restaurant to visit tonight. It'll be dark in less than five minutes, and I'd like to throw up discreetly in a trashcan somewhere. I walk to the edge of the roof and look down. I can see into an alley, and after a moment I realize I'm looking at a leg walking back and forth.

Two days later, Mr. Dinh, a reporter from Houston, will tell me that his son is here somewhere, his adopted son, and I'll think back to the severed leg.

"Not really adopted, you know? Just so we could bring him over, legally, we signed some papers. He lives down here, cuts hair for a living. He has two stepkids. He lived down here. He's been missing since the first day. He's why I took the assignment."

The leg is just a lower leg, ending at the knee. It walks slowly from one side of the alley to the other, never pausing, and its persistence is Mr. Dinh's sorrow. I listen to him talk about his adopted son without quite knowing what to say. There are ghosts everywhere here. I am not imagining the leg, though it would be simpler if I were.

After several days, it becomes clear that I have one advantage over my more credentialed colleagues: I can report what I want. My paper has no parent company to satisfy, no grand, overarching ethos to live up to, no advertisers to worry about offending. And my editor, Hung, is my father.

The majority of Katrina coverage flows in two basic directions. The bad: FEMA's mounting failures, the city's woeful lack of preparation, the Bush Administration's unpardonable inaction. The good: the relief successes, the rebuilding ventures, the happy-ending human-interest features. Families reunited, lives miraculously saved, pets found. The imperative, for the press: at once stoke and assuage the public outrage.

Let the other papers tell those stories. Let NBC's Stone Phillips. Let our version of Stone Phillips, the blandly handsome Mr. Giang, or Đá Phillips, as we like to call him, handle it. I'll write about other things, and my dad will understand. His best gift to his only daughter: reportorial carte blanche.

It's early morning our fifth day in, and we're finishing breakfast. Mr. Đê announces loudly that a *Vulitzer* rides on the news coming out of New Orleans. Mr. Bảo nods without looking up. The Vulitzer Prize, created just this year, honors the best writing by a Viet Am for a Viet Am publication. It's worth next to nothing: only a twenty-five-dollar honorarium and little to no prestige. From the way the others are eyeing one another, though, it's as if we're vying for journalistic immortality.

"Where are you from again, little niece?". Mr. Bảo asks me. We're leaving New Orleans, flying out to Biloxi. He's sipping from a flask.

"Henry, Maryland. Midway between Baltimore and DC."

"Henry, huh? Never heard of it. What paper?"

"*Vietnamese American Gazette: Reporting America's News Today*." I say the second part like a radio announcer.

"Never heard of it."

"Web-based, entirely."

After a moment, he blurts out: "You know, condense your paper's name, and the acronym is *VAGRANT*." He laughs. "Says it all, doesn't it!" He licks his lips, looks down and away. "Just joking. Don't be insulted. Want a cigarette?"

Actually it does say it all. The acronym's no accident. For political and spiritual reasons I don't really want to go into, my dad doesn't consider America a true home. Hence *VAGRANT*: we're all vagrants, he thinks, all still boat people, romantic wanderers, a little like Aeneas after the Trojan War.

"So where'd you get your degree from?" Mr. Bảo asks, fiddling with his shoelaces, clearly bored. He earned his at Việt Nam's prestigious Press and Communication Institute. For years he's worked for the famed *Nguoi Viet Daily News*. He's speaking to me in Vietnamese, and his phrasings aren't the appropriate ones—he keeps referring to himself as a peer, instead of as an older gentleman I've just met. He's flirting with me.

I say the name of a school I didn't attend and he nods, not really caring. In fact I'm an autodidact. I have no formal journalistic experience, other than working for *VAGRANT* part-time for the last few years. No degree, no undergraduate experience other than a few community-college credits here and there. Another reason I'm glad we left Việt Nam. If we'd stayed, there's a good chance I'd be a housewife, or maybe a nanny. A market vendor. There's a long tradition of strong women in Việt Nam, but not too many female-autodidacts-become-newspaper-reporters floating around.

I was only four and a half when we left. I'm not really in a position to draw any parallels between the exodus and this disaster. As for my dad, he's hesitant to draw any. Doesn't want to be irresponsible, he says. *Too different, that and this.*

The mainstream media, meanwhile, draws parallels right and left, as do some of the major Viet Am papers. My current compatriots are as guilty as anyone. Standard headline: VIETNAMESE LOSE ALL, THIS TIME TO KATRINA. I guess it's a basic, understandable impulse, the desire to use one event to think through the other.

Too easy, says Dad. *You can't do it. Can't use the senseless to make sense of the senseless.*

But as I remind him, Congress just earmarked $4.5 million for Gulf Coast–area Viet Ams. Tagged to assign the aid funding? Northern Virginia–based Boat People SOS, a group devoted to helping exodus survivors for the last three decades. Easy or not, the connections are inescapable.

My dad's exodus, 1979: in a cargo hold on a shipping freighter, with me smuggled alongside him.

Mr. Bảo's, 1982: by tugboat. Lost for two turbulent months at sea.

Đá Phillips's, 1984–8: eight different refugee camps in six different countries.

Mr. Đê's, 1977–8: fishing boat hijacked by pirates—twice. Lost a toe.

All of my colleagues journeyed without family, I learn. You impoved the odds of escape by splitting up. Unlike me, most children traveled with their mothers; fathers went alone.

According to Mr. Đê, only half-joking, they all survived on *tánh hiên-ngang*. Machismo.

The same machismo, I think, that makes them so endearing and insufferable now.

Sometimes I look back on the exodus fondly, admits Mr. Bảo.

Survival is the ultimate charge to the ego.

Spotted this morning, painted on a rooftop in Village de L'est, the Vietnamese quarter of New Orleans' Ninth Ward: a poem.

Says Mr. Đê: call it *art in media excessus*, art in the midst of death. Or *art in media diritas*, art in the midst of disaster.

Retorts Mr. Bảo: just call it art. Art is always in the midst of death and disaster.

They start squabbling, and the rest of us call it *roof-art*.

The poem, quickly and roughly translated from the original Vietnamese:

What remains
after the monsoon rains?

The scramble
to fill the flooded beds
with rice seed

and

The rest of the poem is missing, along with the rest of the roof.

Many of the houses we pass over are marked. Rescue teams do it to know which houses to search, which not to bother with. Cleanup teams, in turn, know which houses to scour. *Dead bodies inside.*

This is the nominal meaning. Various theories regarding the greater symbolism circulate.

Say the morbid: the marks turn houses into tombstones, New Orleans into a graveyard.

Say those who fault government inattention: the marks are a census of poverty. Dead? Must be poor.

Or: the marks are a census of race. Dead? Must not be white (unless poor white trash, not-quite-white).

Or: the marks are signs of a nation's guilt.

Or: they stand for grief.

A leg walks back and forth in an alley.

The next morning, the group splits up. *Race starts here, gentlemen*, says Mr. Đê. He means the race for the Vulitzer. I'd all but forgotten, but my colleagues take this very seriously. Part of me would like to win it just so I could throw it away right in front of them. Part of me would like to win it so I could present it to my dad to hang up in his office.

The air is full of mold spores. My father sends his love by email. Anger haunts Village de L'est like a ghost. I interview a man named Jimmy Lê in a half-ruined church, roof gaping open.

(*Roughly translated from the Vietnamese*)

KAREN NGUYỄN: So you were telling me about your financial situation.

JIMMY LÊ: I'm totally wiped out. My business, the building collapsed. My house, it's halfway underwater. And my car, I don't even know where it is. I think it floated off somewhere. [*His hair falls into his eyes. He has a despondent look on his suddenly beautiful face.*] Maybe someone stole it. I think I'd prefer if someone stole it.

KN: What about insurance?

JL: Right now, nothing. I have no proof-of-insurance papers. They're in the house, which is condemned, so I can't go in. [*Pause*] People say the insurance companies will honor the policies even without official papers. After they investigate. But no one's very optimistic.

KN: Where are you staying now? A shelter?

JL: No, everyone in the neighborhood has already gotten FEMA trailers. About two weeks ago. [*He thinks for a moment, and decides to say more*] But something's wrong with them. One of my neighbors has nosebleeds, and we all get headaches. Our eyes itch and our noses won't stop running. They smell like—it's hard to breathe inside after a while, especially when you're sleeping. So, no, the response is no fucking good. Want to see the trailer?

He walks me three short blocks to the lot where his house used to stand. The trailer sits up on concrete stumps in front of the rubbled outline of the house. It's roughly ten feet by thirty, gray, and does in fact smell like chemical waste. The faint, acrid smell of formaldehyde.

But that's not the story. It could be, but it's not.

Twenty minutes later, I learn that there's a man who communes with ghosts working his way around New Orleans. He's a *nhap xac*, a medium. Used to work for the Vietnamese government, searching for the family members of party officials, searching for long-lost

MIAs to appease the U.S. He finds the ghosts, and the ghosts take him to the bodies.

A woman missing half her fingernails tells me this. A salon owner who lives just down the block from Jimmy Lê. The man's name is Chien Xem Ma, she says, "Chien who sees ghosts." He's one of the most famous mediums in all of Việt Nam.

She's looking for her sister's children, two teenagers and a toddler.

Everybody's looking for somebody.

I'm staying in a suite at the fairly swanky Chateau Dupre in the heart of the French Quarter. I was rooming at a Days Inn, but my colleagues pulled some strings and secured an extra room here, free of charge.

I've been told that the late-night knock is a typical feature of the hotel stay in Việt Nam. I experience a similar phenomenon every night here at the Chateau, except instead of young Vietnamese prostitutes, I'm solicited by aging Viet Am reporters.

Mr. Bảo asks sweetly if I might like a nightcap.

Mr. Hien says he has good cocaine.

Mr. Đê tells me his age shouldn't fool me; he's a tiger in bed and has the penis of a nineteen-year-old. No Cialis necessary, he promises.

Đá Phillips shows off his English, slurring angrily through the keyhole: *Me love you long time.*

My father predicted that something like this might happen. *I'd probably do the same thing*, he says. I email him my copy for the day, and he happily posts it. The latest installment of my running column is done, with various features in the works, I report. *Whatever you like, little one*, he says. I go to sleep not feeling much like a serious journalist.

As many as a million boat people died at sea in the '70s, '80s, and '90s. Our ghosts over the ocean are thick like clouds. There are no official estimates yet as to how many have died in New Orleans, Viet Ams or otherwise. I don't know what the number will mean, when I find it.

I wake up early and watch television with the sound off. Cartoons, black-and-white reruns, '80s movies. Anything but CNN coverage.

"What would you do with the $4.5 million, if you won it?" Mr. Bảo asks Mr. Dinh. Breakfast conversation, later that morning. It's 5 a.m., and we're all nursing coffees.

"What?"

"The funding from Congress. That Boat People SOS is handing out."

"I know what money you mean. But what are you talking about, idiot? It's not a lump-sum prize; it'll be divvied up."

"Ha! You're so dumb, little brother. Of course it's going to be divvied up. And it's meaningless that way, everyone knows that. $4.5 million cut up—what are there, around fifty thousand of us down here? Everyone only gets about a hundred dollars. Or if they split it up 'fairly,' then maybe some people get nothing. The more 'deserving' people get five thousand. Still window dressing—what the hell does five thousand dollars do?"

Mr. Dinh has a blank look on his face.

"The whole point," Mr. Bảo continues, warming up now, "the whole point is the *symbolic* value of the money. The outside world hears about the grant, says *Those Viet Ams are set*. And everyone down here hears that big number and imagines for a moment he's hitting the jackpot. So the only real question is: what would you do with the $4.5 million?"

My colleagues proceed to fantasize lovingly. I don't say it aloud—they'd tease me—but I'd channel the money back into *VAGRANT*.

That afternoon I trace a quavering line of refugees across the city, asking if anyone knows anything about the ghost hunter. Quite a few people know someone who knows someone. Over in Biloxi, out in Versailles. Two young men claim to have spoken with him directly, but when I press them, they admit that it was friends of friends who met him, maybe even friends of friends of friends. No word as to where Chien Xem Ma might be found.

Finally, in the late afternoon, I meet an elderly woman who tells me the medium helped her locate her husband's body two weeks ago. He depends upon a guardian spirit, she says, to provide a spiritual impression, a rough map of where the body might be located, complete with landmarks. A frozen lake turned on its side, under a great red-and-white sign—this was the image the spirit provided. A fractured storefront window, the ghost hunter intuited. He found the body in the marsh of a flooded, boxed-in convenience store. He drew me to it like a magnet, she says.

But her story comes wrapped in the baffling of two other stories, immediately following. A middle-aged man claims he found the ghost of his sister with the help of a Tibetan Buddhist rimpoche. A young woman claims a qi gong healer with acute psychic sensitivity led her to the remains of her aunt. Suddenly there are three ghost hunters, maybe more. Every story spins outward.

That night I have dinner with Mr. Dinh. I wonder if he's already heard about the ghost hunter through his various leads. I think about his adopted son. I don't want to give him false hope. I don't want him to beat me to my story.

I tell Mr. Dinh I like his tie, then listen with excruciating care as he describes how his wife picked it out for him. Which reminds him of how they first met, and where they've settled in Houston, their grown children, their retirement plans, the quaint café they plan to open, their favorite memories of their life together. He gives me the full sweep of his sweet, expansive love story.

I force myself to listen. Later, alone in my room, I post content to the *VAGRANT* newswire, to the log of features my dad will review first thing in the morning. No mention of the ghost hunter, not yet. I play back the interviews I've recorded and scratch out an outline, then erase it, then scratch it out again. I can't find my story.

Not one hundred yards away, outside the Chùa Bồ Đề Buddhist Temple, a *USA Today* reporter conducts an interview. It's the next day, a rainy afternoon. I'm on chicory coffee number nine. I have nothing going at the moment, so I ask to sit in, watch, maybe learn something. She shrugs.

JENNY WALTERS-MCKINNON, *USA TODAY*: What did you do for a living before Katrina, Mr. Pham?

PHẠM VĂN HAI: Shrimp-boat operator.

JWM: And—

PVH:—You know, I never hear of Ku Kluck Klan before I come to New Orleans. Very funny guys. One midnight, they showing up around my boat. In Vietnam, white mean mourning, so I'm thinking someone important is dead. [*Pause*] Then they try to set my boat on fire. [*Pause*] So maybe they mourning—for me! I am dead and do not know it yet! [*Laughs*]

JWM: Did you call the police?

PVH [*He looks at her as if the question is patently moronic*]: No. I shoot in the air, chase them away.

JWM: Did they ever come back?

PVH: No! I need help. I wish. I offer them job. Good pay. Free dental.

JWM [*She indulges him with a small smile*]: So tell us about your experience with Katrina. Were you still in New Orleans when the hurricane hit?

PVH: Yes, I am trap in my house. It collapse all around.

JWM [*She perks up slightly*]: You were trapped? For how long?

PVH: One week. My leg is pin under a wall that fall down.

JWM [*She glances over at me, arching her eyebrows*]: Mr. Pham, your leg's in pretty good shape for being pinned under a wall for a week.

PVH [*He frowns and cocks his head to the side to indicate he can't understand her. She repeats her question and, smiling, he raises his hands.*]: Sorry, not understanding you, Miss.

(I ask her if she'd like me to ask him in Vietnamese. Vaguely annoyed, she says yes, okay. I translate, and he says, "Little niece, I understand her perfectly well, but why is she asking about my leg? I'm just having a little fun. I don't know what she wants. I don't want to incriminate myself."

"You can't be incriminated for lying to her," I tell him.

"It's not what you call 'perjury'?"

"Only in court."

He nods, then looks back to her quickly.)

PVH: Sorry, Miss, I meaning to say my wife leg is trap. Get mix-up in English. In Vietnamese language, sometimes you referring to your wife as yourself; "you" can mean you, wife, kids, or whole family.

This linguistic explanation is a flagrant falsehood. Ms. Walters-McKinnon nods, but looks skeptical. I cover my smile and wander away. Two helicopters fly overhead, about a minute apart. Up and down the street, black mold now panels the buildings like wainscoting. It's black aspergillus, the new shadow of the city. Mold and ghosts, the life and unlife of New Orleans. I step under the awning of an abandoned café and have a smoke. By the time I come back to the temple, Ms. Walters-McKinnon has moved on.

"Boy, you Northerners really don't have a sense of humor," Mr. Hai says.

He must be confused. "I'm no Northerner," I tell him. "I was born just outside Saigon." I offer him half of my candy bar.

He laughs. "No, I mean 'Yankee,' as the Americans say."

Oh. I'm waiting for him to tell me why he lied to Ms. Walters-McKinnon, but he doesn't, and when I ask him, he just gives me a humorless grin, then chews his half of the Snickers bar, never breaking my gaze. I ask him about the ghost hunter, whether he's seen him, and he shrugs.

"Seen plenty of ghosts. No ghost hunters."

Another poem spotted. We're flying to a dinner hosted by some local development group. Everyone is drinking heavily, and Vulitzer talk predominates. Mr. Đê supposedly knows several members of the governing panel. *He has the inside line*, someone complains.

The trip's nearly over for me. My dad wants to extend it, but I'm ready to go home. The over-rich food, my squabbling colleagues, the uncooperatively absent ghost hunter—they're all wearing on me. The air is exhausting. I'm missing the *VAGRANT* offices in my dad's basement. I'm missing my spare little studio in Henry.

We're passing over a high-rise building, a ruined, abandoned apartment complex, when we see the poem painted on an upper terrace.

I think it's authored by the same woman. I say woman, the rest say man. We all agree it's the same poet—same handwriting. I'll admit the lettering is vaguely masculine, but I can imagine myself out on that roof painting the poem. I can only imagine the rest of my colleagues, and my dad, and most of the other men I've known, writing HELP.

The poem, translated:

Because grief unites us,
Like the locked antlers of moose
who die on their knees in pairs.

My gut tells me to end here and just move on. The verse certainly stands on its own. But a poem is a contract. She went to the trouble of painting it. I'm compelled to add a note.

Later that night I Google the lines and find they're from an old William Matthews poem, "Why We Are Truly a Nation." Hence the perfect translation: I take the lines verbatim from a version posted online, rather than attempting my own reworking of the Vietnamese on the roof, itself a rough reworking of the original English.

So our ghostly poet is a capable translator. And a borrower. Which somehow doesn't ruin anything for me—it seems appropriate, in fact.

Why not summon up Matthews's verse? Describe a new nation, a new grief, a new collective death?

A double-knock at my hotel-room door that night: Mr. Bảo and Mr. Đê, together. Very creepy.

"Care for a nightcap?"

I sigh. "What about your wives, gentlemen?"

"Back in Việt Nam." The way Mr. Bảo says it—wistfully, looking for a moment over to Mr. Đê —one can't be sure whether their wives couldn't or wouldn't come over.

"My mom never made it here either," I say.

"Ah." After a respectful pause, Mr. Bảo looks down at the bottle of whiskey he's holding, then back at me, then back at the bottle.

I shake my head. "I'm the daughter you teach to avoid old lechers like you two."

"I never taught my daughter any such thing," Mr. Đê retorts quickly. But even for him, the mood has sobered irrevocably.

They stay until around 1 a.m., Mr. Bảo and I drinking whiskey in the dark, Mr. Đê taking out his dentures and rubbing Mr. Hien's cocaine on his gums, all of us smoking, the TV on with the sound turned up high enough to discourage conversation. Mr. Bảo rubs his lap absentmindedly. I wonder what the ghost hunter is doing at this precise moment. It's agonizing to know that he's out there somewhere, no more than a short taxi ride away—as is the mystery poet. One of them, I am convinced, offers the only real measure of peace available. The only way of making sense of this mess, doing what the official programs and the visiting aid workers, however well-intentioned, cannot.

When *The Tonight Show* finishes, Mr. Đê and Mr. Bảo glide off without a word.

My dad used to tell me a story about my uncle Quan, whom everyone called *người đi lắc lư*. He lived on a houseboat on Ha Long Bay, where he worked as a fisherman. All day long, every day of his life, he sat and fished, or sat and rowed, or swam, or crawled like a crab from bow to stern, boat to boat. He stood and walked so little that his body eventually forgot how. *Người đi lắc lư*: a wobbler.

But boy, you should have seen him swim, says my dad. We can adapt to anything, he wanted me to realize. I was set to start American kindergarten the next day.

I have my uncle Quan's story in mind when I interview a man named Lưu Lâm Phuc, a self-identified looter. He wants to be found, is seeking out interviews. He doesn't ask that his name be changed or withheld; he's proud of his looting. Fancies himself a *Rowbin Huit*. A Robin Hood.

Mr. Dinh, who's with me when I meet Mr. Phuc, wants nothing to do with him. *Nutbag for sure*, he says. None of the others want anything to do with Mr. Phuc. He stinks of wood-fire smoke and maybe chemical fumes. He won't look away from you once he's made eye contact. I imagine that no one wants anything to do with this guy.

(*Translated from the Vietnamese*)

KAREN NGUYỄN: Before we get into the looting, can you tell me briefly about your experience on the boats, your journey to the U.S.?

LƯU LÂM PHUC: My family and I got out in 1983.

KN: Can you say any more?

LLP: We stopped at a refugee camp in Malaysia. [*Pause. I wait, but he doesn't add anything.*]

KN: Do you see any parallels between then and now?

LLP [*Speaking immediately, no pause, and flatly, without affect*]: Most of all the feeling. The helicopters fly overhead but don't stop. The boats pass by but never let you aboard. Hopelessness. Lawlessness—no law once you're out on the water, then or now. Anything goes.

KN: Have you? Let "anything go"?

LLP [*He squints*]: Yes.

KN: So the looting—what have you taken? From where?

LLP: Anything I needed. From stores, houses, abandoned houses.

KN: Can you be more specific?

[*He shrugs, shakes his head slightly*]

KN: Do you believe what you've doing is right? Justifiable?

LLP: Then or now?

KN: Either one.

LLP: Yes. And yes. [*He smiles a crooked, crazed smile. There's blood in his mouth, several of his upper teeth boxed in dark red. I think for sure he's not only hurt people, but hurt without remorse, perhaps even with pleasure.*] I'm *Rowbin Huit*.

KN: Are you worried about legal repercussions?

LLP: No. I do it in broad daylight. [*Long pause. He takes out a cigarette but doesn't light it. With his boyish face and ragged pompadour, he looks like some kind of ruined imitation of James Dean. I keep thinking,* tánh hiên-ngang, tánh hiên-ngang.]

KN: What will you do when conditions return to normal?

[*Long look, as if the question is patently moronic. Then he shrugs. Makes to stand up and leave.*]

KN: Wait, one last question.

LLP: Go ahead.

KN: Have you seen a gh—I mean, do you have any daughters?

On my last night here, my colleagues try to take me out and get me drunk. They can really drink, and they're in the right place: bars have survived everywhere. Actually, they've been out drinking nearly every night—this is just my first time going with them. The whole trip has been one raucous bender, for them, which may seem a little strange, given the circumstances, but then each of my colleagues remembers the exodus with nostalgia. Katrina junket as class reunion. The Vulitzer will be awarded in several weeks. I'd like to say I don't care who wins.

How does the trip end? Maybe I notice something that boozy, sweaty night at the bars, or on the early flight out the next morning.

Maybe from the window I spot, dot-sized, far below, the mystery poet at her work on a rooftop. End by transcribing her newest poem, fade out with some profundity.

Maybe the ghost hunter leaves on the same plane.

No such luck. No neat ending.

I'm going back in three months. I have an appointment to interview Mr. Phuc's daughter. That's my ending.

AFTERWORLD

by ANTHONY DOERR

1

IN A TALL HOUSE in a yard of thistles eleven girls wake on the floor of eleven bedrooms. Up and down the surrounding blocks, terrace houses stand in four- and five-story rows. In some, roofs have collapsed. In others, façades have crumbled away to reveal inner beams, empty rooms, green pools of rainwater. The few windows that still have glass in their frames reflect back rectangles of sky.

Saplings grow from ruptures in the street. Flights of pink-rimmed clouds sail overhead.

Inside, a three-year-old named Anita Weiss calls hello down the stairwell. Twice, three times. One story below, another girl replies. Two older girls go from floor to floor, bringing the little ones downstairs. Five-year-old Ilouka Croner. Eight-year-old Bela Cohn. Inga Hoffman and Hanelore Goldschmidt and her older sister Regina. Nearsighted Else Dessau.

On the ground floor they find no furniture, no toilets, no doors on the cupboards, no draperies over the windows. The sinks are unplumbed. Ulcerations of paint blister the walls. House martins loop past cracked windowpanes. The girls sit in what was once a parlor in the strengthening daylight. All wear dresses of mismatched sizes. Most are barefoot. Some yawn; some rub their eyes. Some flex their arms and fingers as if they have been fitted with new limbs.

One asks, "Where are we?"

The youngest peer out into the thistles. The oldest frown and search their memories. Several sense something recently settled there, something ghastly, something that might come alive if they poke at it too much.

Nine-year-old Hanelore Goldschmidt treads down the staircase with her hands cupped in front of her. She scans the faces in the parlor.

"Where's Esther? Is Esther here?"

No one answers. A tiny paw, poking out between Hanelore's fingers, trembles visibly.

Inga Hoffman says, "Is that a mouse?"

Else Dessau says, "Has anyone seen my glasses?"

Regina Goldschmidt says, "They can bite, you know."

Hanelore whispers into her hands.

Regina says, "Keep it away from the little ones."

Several of the girls glance continually toward the doorways, expecting Frau Cohen with her housedress and apron to stride in and clap her hands. Get a broom, she'd say. Get a mop. She who rests rusts. Breakfast will be served in twenty minutes. Her skirts smelling of camphor. Four dozen of her cabbage rolls browning in a skillet.

But Frau Cohen does not come through the doorway.

The last to come downstairs is sixteen-year-old Miriam Ingrid Bergen. She walks to the front door and opens it and stands looking out. In the dawn light a block away, through the haphazard trestle of saplings, a single doe steps lightly. It pauses; it twitches its long ears toward Miriam. Then it steps behind a tree and vanishes.

No entryway, no front walk. No paths trampled through the thistles. There are only the blank faces of the neighboring houses and lank curtains of ivy dangling from gutters and a single gull sailing over the broken street. And the light, which seems to carry thousands of miles before it passes over the rooftops in an obliterating silence.

Miriam turns. "We're dead," she says. "I'm sure of it."

2

Esther Gramm is born in 1927 in Hamburg, Germany. Her mother's labor is long and harrowing. For several minutes Esther is trapped inside the birth canal without oxygen. Her mother dies of complications; Esther is left with a quarter-inch scar inside her left temporal lobe.

Her father drowns in a canal four years later. Esther is bundled across the city at night: snow over the jetties, vapor rising from the holes in sewer lids. One-horse carriages scuttle along through the falling white.

The Hirschfeld Trust Girls' Orphanage at Number 30 Papendam is a five-story row house in a middle-class Jewish neighborhood. In its dormitories a dozen girls sleep on folding cots. They wear their hair in tandem plaits; they wear matching black stockings and shin-length dresses. They walk to gymnastics class on Tuesday evenings, repair their clothes on Wednesday evenings, weave matzoh baskets on Thursday evenings. Every morning the House Directress, Frau Cohen, listens to the girls read in synchrony from donated readers. *Little Solomon is sweeping the coal bin. Little Isaac is pulling his wagon.*

Esther has been at Number 30 Papendam for a year when she begins having epileptic seizures. She smells an overwhelming smell of celery when none is present. Or a sense of impending annihilation swamps her and for a full minute she cannot respond to anything anyone says. Her feet and hands tingle; she clenches her fists repeatedly; she soaks through her dress with sweat.

Months later, when Esther is six, she is sitting in the washroom in a chair beside the three iron bathtubs, waiting her turn for a bath, when she hears what sounds like a steam engine rumble to life in the distance. Within seconds the train sounds as if it has drawn close enough to explode through the wall. None of the other girls glance up. Frau Cohen carries in a stack of folded nightdresses, her sleeves rolled up, three strands of hair hanging over her eyes. She looks at Esther and tilts her head slightly. Her mouth moves, but no sound comes out.

Esther clamps her palms over her ears. The train roars as if through the throat of a tunnel. In an instant it will be upon her; in an instant she will be crushed. Then the train passes through her head.

Here is what the other girls see: little Esther slips off the chair in the corner, lands on her side on the tile, and starts convulsing. Her wrists curl inward. Her eyes blink a dozen times a second.

Here is what Esther sees: an unfurnished room. The train is gone, the girls are gone, Hirschfeld House is gone. Violet, snow-refracted light washes through two windows. A man and woman sit cross-legged on the floor. For a moment they look together up through a window. Snow blows past apartment houses across the street.

"First we die," the woman says. "Then our bodies are buried. So we die two deaths."

Esther can feel, distantly, that her body is kicking.

"Then," continues the woman, "in another world, folded inside the living world, we wait. We wait until everyone who knew us when we were children has died. And when the last one of them does, we die our third death."

Out the window wind catches the snow and seems to blow it upward, back into the clouds.

"That's when we're released to the next world," the woman says. In the Hirschfeld House bathroom, one of the girls screams. Frau Cohen drops the stack of nightdresses. Maybe nine seconds pass. Esther wakes up.

3

Seventy-five years later, eighty-one-year-old Esther Gramm finds herself flat on her back in her garden in Geneva, Ohio. She is a widow, a grower of prize-winning carrots, and a mildly celebrated illustrator of children's books. She lives alone in a pale blue house on thirteen acres of maples and poplars four miles from Lake Erie. She has lived here for fifty years.

Esther's son and his blond, cross-country-skiing wife live next door in a white colonial on the other side of a wall of willows. Four days ago they flew to Changsha, China, to adopt twin girls. There have been visa problems, an unexpected bungling of documents. Suddenly everything is in question. Their son, Robert—a college junior home for the summer—has told his grandmother that his parents may have to remain in China for several weeks.

Esther's left hand is clamped in her grandson's right. Her whole body is damp with sweat. The windows of her house, visible between the slats of her garden fence, glow lightly against the dusk. Robert presses his fist into his forehead. "Four this week," he says.

"They're real," Esther whispers. She sits up too quickly and her eyesight flees in long streaks. Robert retrieves her eyeglasses, helps her to her feet.

"We're going to the hospital," he says. Clouds of gnats throb against the sky. The first bats whirl out of the trees.

"No." Esther shuts her eyes—they feel strangely untethered. She has not experienced seizures like this, fully generalized absence episodes, since she was fifteen years old. "No hospital."

She leans on him as they cross the lawn. He lays her on her couch; he stabs buttons on his little black telephone.

"Dad?" says Robert. "Dad?" A dull pressure pulses against Esther's temples.

"I saw it again," she whispers. "A tall house in a yard of thistles."

"It was a seizure, Grandmom," Robert says, peering into the screen of his phone. "You were only out for nine seconds. I timed it start to finish. You were in the garden the whole time."

"It felt like hours," Esther mumbles. "It felt like all day."

"Dad," says Robert, talking into the phone now. "She had another one." Robert explains, nods, explains some more. Then he passes the phone to Esther so she can listen to her son berate her from eight thousand miles away. She must go to the neurology clinic in Cleveland, he says. He says she is being pigheaded, stubborn, impossible. She says she is stronger than he is six days a week.

"Think about Robert, Mom." His voice is close, cracking; he sounds as if he might still be next door. But Esther is thinking of the clinic—of palsied faces riding elevators in chrome wheelchairs. Cartoon-character bedscreens behind which rest the shaved heads of children.

"This whole thing is such a fuckup," says her son. "Maybe we should just come home."

"You handle your problems," says Esther. "I'll handle mine."

She hands the phone back. Robert presses END. They eat scrambled eggs in the dimness of the kitchen. Fireflies drift and flash in the amphitheater of her huge backyard. Robert says, "Promise me. If you have one more, we'll go."

Esther looks over at him. Five-foot-two Robert in his Cleveland

Browns sweatshirt and Army shorts and flip-flops, forking in mouthfuls of eggs. The boy has been recording interviews with Esther over the past several weeks for reasons she doesn't fully understand. Something to do with history classes in college. A thesis, he calls it. "Okay," she says. "I promise."

Robert walks home. Esther feels her way down the hall and climbs into bed fully clothed. Her brain swings and bangs inside her skull. These past weeks she has been sensing shapes flowing beneath the objects of her room; what might be violin music sifts now and then out of the walls. Her senses seem to have grown more acute: when she leans on her elbows in her garden she can see the leaves unfurl, and thicken, and shine. She does not want to cook, or weed, or read. Yesterday she walked the long driveway to the mailbox in a slow drizzle and paused with her hand on the fence and sat down in the gravel and stared up, letting the rain fall into her eyes, and was certain for a long moment that she could sense a silvery, restless world rippling just beneath this one.

Now, in her bedroom at 9 p.m., with the lamp switched off, streams of unbidden memories rise—decades old, deeply buried. She hears the bustle and rush of Hirschfeld House, feet scrambling down the stairs, dresses flapping on lines in the garden, dance music streaming out of the big, walnut-paneled wireless Radiola Five in the parlor. Every Sabbath for eleven years Esther took her place at the long refectory table and looked from the backs of her hands to the backs of the hands of the other girls, Miriam and Regina and Hanelore and Else, all of them arrayed around the table in prayer. Time compresses; Esther blinks into the darkness and wonders for a long moment if she is no longer in Ohio at all, but back inside the row house at Number 30 Papendam, more than sixty years ago, a dozen girls on two benches, a dozen young hearts thrumming beneath their sweaters, three blue streetlamps swaying in the wind outside the windows.

4

With a key Dr. Rosenbaum scratches the soles of six-year-old Esther's feet; with a silver reflector he gazes into her pupils. He listens carefully to her description of the man and the woman and the snow blowing upward.

"Fascinating, these hallucinations," he murmurs. "Do you think she could be imagining her parents?"

Frau Cohen frowns; she does not like fanciful talk. "Is it the falling sickness?"

"Maybe," the doctor says. "More fat in her diet. Fewer sugars. Let's not pack her into the asylum just yet."

Two weeks after her seizure in the bathroom, Esther has another. Again she finds herself watching a man and a woman in an unfurnished house. This time they pad down a stairwell into a twilit city. They wind between canyons of terrace houses for what seems like several hours, joining a slow march of others out in the cold. Everyone moves in the same direction, toward a forest at the edge of the city. Snow lands on the shoulders of their coats and gathers in the brims of their hats.

Dr. Rosenbaum prescribes a bitter-smelling anticonvulsant called phenobarbital. It comes in a jar the size of Esther's fist. A glass dropper is slotted through the lid. Esther is supposed to swallow six drops three times a day.

A month passes. Then another. Sometimes Esther feels slow and glassy; sometimes she finds it impossible to sit still during lessons. But the drug works: her moods stabilize; her mind does not derail.

Miriam Ingrid Bergen, a long-waisted seven-year-old with a delicate chin and a penchant for risk, takes Esther under her wing. She shows her where Frau Cohen keeps her tobacco, which bakeries will hand out scraps of dough; she explains which boys in the market are trustworthy and which are not. Together the two of them stand in the Hirschfeld House bathroom and stack their hair in various arrangements and draw ink around the rims of their eyes and laugh into the mirror until their ribs ache.

Esther spends much of the rest of her time drawing. She sketches ancient cities, tattooed giants, banners fluttering from spires. She draws fifty-story bell towers, torch-lined tunnels, bridges made from thread, strange amalgamations of imagination and what feels peculiarly like memory.

She turns seven; she turns eight. One month, it seems, no one in Hamburg is wearing armbands, and the next month practically everyone is. Photos in Reich newspapers show soldiers on parade, tanks draped in roses, plantations of flags. In one picture six German fighter bombers fly in formation, wingtip to wingtip, suspended above a mountain range of clouds. Eight-year-old Esther studies it. Spangles of sun flash from the windshields. Each pilot leans slightly forward. As if glory is a lamp dangling just beyond the blades of the propellers.

On Esther's ninth birthday Dr. Rosenbaum arrives with nine pencils wrapped in ribbon. "Growing up so tall," he marvels. He replenishes Esther's bottle of anticonvulsant; he asks her a series of questions about her latest illustrations. He looks for a long time at a drawing in which a miniature city sprouts from the head of a pin: tiny rooftops covered with tinier tiles, tiny flags waving from infinitesimal spires.

"Extraordinary," he declares.

At dinner all the girls sit as close as they can to Dr. Rosenbaum's wife, a tiny woman with bright silver hair who smells of cashmere and perfume. She tells the girls about bridges over the Arno, apiaries in the Luxembourg Gardens, sailboats in the Aegean. After the meal the oldest girls serve cake on the Hirschfeld House tea set, and everyone gathers around Frau Rosenbaum in the parlor to examine her picture postcards: Stockholm, London, Miami. Spiderwebs of rain fall past the windows. Violin music whispers out of the big Radiola Five. Frau Rosenbaum describes the November light in Venice, how it simultaneously hardens and softens everything.

"In the evenings that light is like liquid," she sighs. "You want to drink it."

Esther closes her eyes and sees archways, canals, staircases coiling around mile-high towers. She sees a man and a woman crouched in front of a window, cross-hatchings of snow falling beyond the glass.

When she opens her eyes, a crow is sitting on a branch just outside the parlor window. It turns an eye toward her, cocks its head, blinks. Esther walks toward it, sets her palm against a pane. Does she see it? Just there? Something glowing between its feathers? Some other world folded inside this one?

The crow flaps away. The branch bobs.

Frau Rosenbaum murmurs another story; the girls sigh and giggle. Esther looks out into the night and thinks: We wait. We wait until everyone who knew us when we were children has died.

5

Eighty-one-year-old Esther wakes at 6 a.m. and has to lean against the wall as she walks to the bathroom. Her whole house seems to teeter back and forth, as though in the night someone has towed it four miles north and set it adrift upon the swells of Lake Erie.

The sun rises. She makes herself toast but has no appetite for it. Out in the garden a rabbit sits chewing, but Esther cannot muster the effort to scare it away. Just now her stomach feels as if it is pulsing, as if hornets are convening inside it.

All her adult life, memory has been her enemy. Her childhood was something to be sealed off, put out of mind. Now it seems to refuse any efforts to tuck it away; memories stream out of the walls, out of the sky, out of the soil.

A train roars to life in the distance. Esther kneels, then falls onto her side. She seizes.

In something like a dream, Esther watches Miriam Ingrid Bergen lead Hanelore Goldschmidt up the stairwell of a tall, narrow house.

Three flights, four flights. The rooms they pass have nothing in them. At the top of the stairwell Miriam pushes through a trapdoor into an attic. Through twin hexagonal windows in the dormers, they peer out.

Dangling fire escapes, truncated chimneys, rusted ducting. A narrow canal choked with trees. All the rooftops have weeds sprouting from between tiles; some have caved in entirely. No smoke. No trams, no lorries, no generators, no whanging hammers or clopping horses or shouting children. No surface clatter. No sheets of newsprint flying in the wind.

"Is this Hamburg?" whispers Hanelore.

Miriam doesn't answer. She is looking at a distant building perhaps twenty stories tall: the tallest building she can see. From its roof a steel-lattice radio antenna anchored with guy wires rises still higher; at its very summit a single green beacon flashes.

A flock of small black birds wheels slowly around it.

"Where is everybody?" asks Hanelore.

"I don't know," says Miriam.

They return downstairs. The other girls sit against the walls, wordless and afraid and a bit hungry. Sand in their eyes. The smaller ones nodding off again. Phrases flutter between them. "No matches?" "What about supper?" "How can there be no one?" The wind, washing through the cracked windows, carries the smell of seawater. The big, empty house moans. The thistles creak.

Esther wakes up. She has another generalized seizure in her

bathroom at noon. And a third in the kitchen around dusk. Each time she sees the girls she lived with as a child. They drink from a nearby canal; they collect crab apples and carry them back to the house in the pulled-up hems of their dresses. They go to sleep shivering on the floor in front of the cold hearth.

After dark Esther finds herself in her bed not entirely sure how she got there. There is a smell in the air like dust, like old paper, like nothing alive. Leaves swish against the gutters of her house, a sound like lapping water. She cannot remember if she has eaten anything since breakfast. She knows she should call Robert, but the energy to sit up and reach for the telephone will not come. Some part of her wishes she could stay in that other world, that she didn't have to go through the trouble of coming back into her eighty-one-year-old self. So much time has passed. And yet the urge to hold Miriam's hand is as strong within her now as it was seventy years ago.

Out her window, clouds blow past stars. On their huge undersides she imagines she can see the reflected wash of an antenna beacon as it flashes green, green, green.

6

Autumn in Hamburg, 1937, and the house martins depart for the Sahara. The storks, Dr. Rosenbaum has told Esther, will travel all the way to South Africa. While all through the country Jewish people are hurrying north, in the opposite direction, toward the ports.

Signs sprout outside the butcher's, outside the theater, outside Schlösser's restaurant, always painted in the same trim calligraphy. *Juden sind hier unerwünscht*. No walks for pleasure. No smiling. No eye contact. These rules are not written down, but they might as well be.

Esther is ten when the first emigration letter arrives. "The German-Israelite Community Office has arranged for Nancy to be emigrated to Warsaw," Frau Cohen announces. Several girls clap; others hold their hands over their mouths. Everyone looks at Nancy, who chews her bottom lip.

Auswanderung: it means emigration. To Esther the word evokes images of butterfly migrations, desert nomads rolling up tents, the long, unpinned chevrons of geese that pass over the house in autumn. When she thinks of Warsaw she imagines grand palaces, silver candlesticks, food carts rattling through ballrooms. She draws streetlamps reflected in a river and a four-wheeled carriage pulled by two white horses bedecked in bells. A trim driver with a tasseled whip rides on the box, and inside a little girl in long gloves sits behind a veil of silk.

Two dawns later, fourteen-year-old Nancy Schwartzenberger stands in the hall clutching a cardboard suitcase nearly as big as she is. Inside she has crammed her Hebrew reader, several dresses, three pairs of stockings, two loaves of bread, and a china plate left to her by her deceased mother. Her carefully handwritten luggage tag is looped through the handle.

The remaining Hirschfeld girls crowd the top of the second-story stairwell, still in their nightdresses, the older ones holding up the youngest so they can see. Down in the parlor Nancy is small in a white cardigan and navy blue dress. She looks as if she cannot make up her mind whether to laugh or to cry.

Frau Cohen walks her to the deportation center and comes back alone. A single letter comes from Nancy in October. *I'm sowing buttons all day. The men I came with are lyeing pavement for motorrways. This work is hard. Its awful crowded. I'd die for a latke. Bles you all.*

Through the ensuing winter rumors swirl through Hirschfeld House like tendrils of some invisible gas. The girls hear that all stores owned by Jewish people will be ransacked; they hear that the government is preparing a weapon called the Secret Signal that turns the brains of every Jewish kid to paste. They hear policemen are slipping into Jewish houses at night and shitting on dining room tables while everyone is asleep.

Each girl becomes a carrier of her own individual measure of hope, fear, and superstition. Else Dessau says the Foreign Exchange Department is allowing steamships crammed with children called *Kindertransports* to travel to England. Before departing, they may go to any department store in the city and select three traveling outfits. Regina Goldschmidt says the police are taking all the handicapped people in Hamburg to a brick house behind the Hamburg-Eppendorf hospital and sitting them in special chairs that shoot their private parts with rays. Epileptics, too, she says, and looks straight at Esther.

Gold and silver are confiscated. Driver's licenses are confiscated. Smoked herring disappears; butter and fruit become memories. Frau Cohen starts rationing paper, and Esther has to resort to drawing on the edges of newspapers and in the margins of books. She draws an ogre closing a butterfly net over a platter-sized city; she draws a gargantuan crow crushing row houses in its beak.

Esther and Miriam hold hands between their cots in the winter darkness and Esther whispers destinations into the space above their beds: Argentina, Antarctica, Australia.

"I hope," Esther says, "we are sent together."

"Only children from the same family," Miriam says, "get sent together."

Surely, Esther believes, they will be welcomed somewhere. She imagines Nancy Schwartzenberger sitting down after a day's work with a dozen others, steaming dishes passing from one hand to the next. She draws the lights of chandeliers reflected in sparkling tableware. And every two months Dr. Rosenbaum comes by to listen to her heart and look at her drawings and replenish her bottle of phenobarbital.

In November of 1938 she and Miriam sit inside the neighborhood druggist's in a leatherette booth with three squares of chocolate between them. It's the first time Frau Cohen has allowed them out of Hirschfeld House in four days. Every customer who enters seems to know something new: the synagogues are going to be burned tomorrow; the Jewish Shipping Company will be Aryanized; all the adult males in the neighborhood will be arrested.

An elderly man runs in and claims that boys in jackboots and armbands are breaking windows in a shoe shop on Benderstrasse. The drugstore goes quiet. Within ten minutes, the remaining customers have slipped out. Esther can feel a familiar, slow apprehension coiling itself around her throat.

"We should go," she tells Miriam.

The overweight druggist sits down in a booth across from them. His face looks as pale and hard as a pebble of quartz. Every now and then he emits an audible whimper.

"Who's he talking to?" Miriam whispers.

The druggist stares into nothing. Outside a gang of boys pedal past, bunched over their bicycles, one trailing a long crimson flag. Esther takes her bottle of anticonvulsant from her pocket and sets three drops onto the back of her tongue.

The druggist's telephone, mounted to the wall behind the counter, rings five, six times. The druggist's attention flips from the telephone to the window.

"Why won't he answer the telephone?"

"Can we go?" whispers Esther. "I don't feel well."

"Something's wrong with him."

"Please, Miriam."

The phone rings. The girls watch. And as they do the druggist takes a razor out of his pocket and cuts his own throat.

7

Esther is riding with Robert in his father's Nissan on the way to Foodtown when she hears a train explode to life off to her right. By reflex she glances out the passenger window across Route 20, where no cars are coming and no trains have run for decades—a pleasant midmorning light falls onto a weedy roadside lot—and her legs stiffen and the smell in the car suddenly turns sour and the streetlights appear to flare and then wink out.

Esther comes back to her senses inside the neurology center in Cleveland. A plastic EEG recording cap, studded with dozens of wired electrodes, is installed on her head. Robert sleeps in the corner chair with the hood of his sweatshirt pulled up and the strings drawn so tightly that only his nose and mouth are visible.

A nurse in a blue smock tells Esther she has had an absence that lasted almost three hours. "But you're here now," she says, and pats the back of Esther's hand.

When he's awake, Robert plays some sort of videogame on the screen of his phone, sketches in a spiral notebook, or watches quiz shows on the television mounted in the corner. Twice he has long, one-sided telephone conversations with his parents in China. She's okay, Dad. She's right here. They're doing tests.

In the evening a redheaded neurologist sits beside Esther's bed. Robert reads from questions he has written down in block printing on the torn scraps of a grocery bag. The doctor offers even-tempered answers. The lesion inside Esther's hippocampus, he says, is almost twice as large as the last time they scanned it. They don't know why it's growing, but it's surely responsible for the onset of her convulsions. They plan to adjust her medications, increase dosages, introduce neuroactive steroids. They will need to observe her for a week. Possibly longer.

Esther hears little of this. Everything looks watery and remote right now; the drugs make her feel as if she is looking out at the world through flooded goggles. Time drifts. She listens to Robert's electronic game as it emits its anesthetic beeps. Among the ceiling tiles she watches barefoot girls tear small pink crab apples from trees. They eat quickly, ravenously. They move about pale and strange in their undergarments with the ladders of their ribs showing. They shamble along broken streets, the smallest of them tripping now and then because her shoes are too large. And then they are gradually subsumed by fog and an unwavering, internal thudding, whether of her heart or of some intramural hospital machinery, Esther cannot say.

Around midnight Robert leaves Esther and drives the Nissan fifty miles back to Geneva and sits in his parents' big kitchen alone. His college friends are hundreds of miles away and he has not stayed in touch with high school friends from town. He should probably be reading history books, working on his thesis, editing the interviews he has already recorded with his grandmother. Instead he eats a bowl of canned soup and pages through a children's book Esther illustrated years ago: a princess who lives in a palace of ice. Out in the yard moonlight spills through the trees.

His mother calls from China to say that his grandmother will need things: toothbrush, cholesterol pills, underwear, something to read. "Underwear?" repeats Robert, and his mother, sitting on a folding chair in a government-run transition house in Changsha at 2 p.m., says, "Just do it, Robert."

Moths flutter against Esther's porch light. The entry hall feels damp and empty. Robert wipes his shoes; he walks through his grandmother's kitchen for perhaps the thousandth time. But it feels desolate tonight; it feels as if something vital has been stripped out of it.

He packs a blouse, some pants, a pair of slippers. On the table beside her bed is a novel, and sticking out of its pages is a sheet of paper the size of an index card. Robert tugs the card free.

On one side is a smudged pencil drawing: a house with weeds growing out of its gutters. Five stories, two gables. Around the foundation more weeds flow outward into a broken, overgrown street.

On the other side of the card are the names and birthdates of twelve girls. It looks old: the paper is yellow, the text gray.

Name, reads the row across the top, then *Date of Birth*, *Date of Deportation*, and *Destination*. For each name, the dates of deportation and the destinations are the same. *July 29, 1942. Birkenau.*

Robert reads the names from top to bottom. *Ellen Scheurenberg. Bela Cohn. Regina Goldschmidt. Hanelore Goldschmidt. Anita Weiss. Zita Dettmann. Inga Hoffman. Gerda Kopf. Else Dessau. Miriam Ingrid Bergen. Esther Gramm.*

8

In August of 1939, another Hirschfeld girl—Ella Lefkovits—is deported to Romania. She is seven years old. A week later Mathilde Seidenfeld receives her own summons: she is being sent east with a cousin to a place called Theresienstadt. "They say it's a spa town," Mathilde murmurs. On her last unmarked sheets of paper Esther draws avenues lined with steaming pools, marble bathhouses, crystal globes glowing on top of brass poles. She writes *For Mathilde* across the bottom, tucks the drawings into Mathilde's suitcase.

In nightmares Esther burns. Flames chew through the draperies of the dormitories; the druggist gulps wetly as he slumps over in his leatherette booth. No letters come from either Ella or Mathilde. By now three new, younger orphans have replaced the deported girls at Number 30 Papendam; two of them are infants. Everyone speaks quietly; up and down Papendam passersby glance periodically toward the sky, as if they're being hunted from the air.

Germany bombs London; Esther turns thirteen. She swallows her doses of anticonvulsant; she cranks in laundry from the lines in the garden. She listens to the distant sounds of ship whistles and the ringing of the harbor cranes. She speaks to Miriam all the time now about far-away places: Kathmandu, Bombay, Shanghai. Miriam seldom replies.

In September a newspaper notice demands that all Jewish-owned radio sets be delivered to collection centers by the twenty-third. Two nights later the twelve Hirschfeld girls gather in the parlor with Frau Cohen, Dr. and Frau Rosenbaum, and Julius, the old custodian, to listen to one last broadcast on the Radiola Five. State programming plays an opera from Berlin. The girls perch on the sofas and along the floor with their legs crossed beneath them. The house fills with a grand, staticky voice.

Frau Cohen holds a sleeping baby. Dr. Rosenbaum paces. Frau Rosenbaum sits with her back very straight and closes her eyes for the entire performance. Every now and then she inhales deeply, as if the speaker were emitting some rare fragrance.

Afterward the girls remain seated as Julius unplugs the Radiola, loads it onto a dolly, and thumps it down the front steps. Where the radio once stood remains a rectangle of floorboards less faded than the rest.

9

In the clinic in Cleveland Esther drifts through dizzy, medicated hours. The steroids will prevent edema, the neurologist says; the anticonvulsants will prevent more seizures.

Robert stands over her at what might be noon of her third day there with a sheet of watercolor paper and a fistful of pencils. All his life they have drawn together; as a boy he'd sit in her lap and they'd draw superheroes, spaceships, pirate galleons. He used to spend hours peering into the framed drawings Esther had hung around her house; he'd grown up reading children's stories she had illustrated. Mice tramping upright through a torchlit tunnel. Lost princesses ferrying lanterns through a forest. Now Robert pivots his grandmother's eating tray across her midsection; he props up her back with a pillow and fits the arms of her glasses over her ears.

It takes Esther a full ten seconds to coax her fingers into picking up a pencil. Robert watches patiently, standing beside her, his head tilted.

With great effort she brings the pencil to paper. In her mind she pictures a white house, eleven girls peering out of eleven windows. She traces a single line across the page. Time passes. She manages another line, then two more: a lopsided rectangle.

When she holds the paper up to the lenses of her glasses, it's a welter of faint crisscrosses. Nothing resolves out of it.

"Grandmom?" asks Robert.

Esther looks at him through tears.

10

The house cook disappears. Julius the custodian is sent to a labor camp. No letters come from either of them. By now Frau Cohen is spending several hours a day in ration queues, deportation request queues, and paperwork queues. The oldest girls prepare meals; the younger ones wash dishes. Esther draws steamships in the margins of old newspapers: four fat smokestacks, crowds at the railings, porters on the ramps.

In the fall of 1941, when Esther is fourteen years old, Dr. Rosenbaum misses an appointment with her for the first time. Frau Cohen sends Miriam and Esther to his clinic. The girls walk quickly, fingers interlaced; every few blocks Esther swallows back an upsurge of panic.

At his little ground-floor office the doctor's bronze nameplate has been pried off the wall. Through a side window the girls stand between hedges and watch a fumigator pump clouds of gas into what had been his examination room. The carpet has been rolled up; the cupboard doors are gone.

"They've emigrated," decides Frau Cohen. "They are well-connected people and it was probably fairly easy for them. They waited as long as they could, and then they fled." She looks Esther in the eye. "Stay busy. You'll be with us."

Esther thinks: He would have told me. He would not have left without telling me. She peers into her jar of phenobarbital. Inside is enough medicine to last maybe two weeks.

She tries three different apothecaries. Two won't let her enter; the last asks for her name, address, and identification papers. Esther scurries out of the shop. She rations herself to three drops a day. Then two. Then one.

Unexpectedly, her brain begins to feel quicker, electrified. A night passes in which all she does is draw by candlelight. Twenty thousand cross-hatchings of pencil, dark cities full of rain, pale figures moving down snowy streets, only a few circles of white on the paper to represent streetlights. Draw the darkness, Esther thinks, and it will point out the light which has been in the paper all the while. Inside this world is folded another.

Hour by hour, day by day, her senses sharpen as her moods destabilize. She feels giddy, then anxious; she yells at Else Dessau for taking too long in the bathroom; she yells at Miriam for no reason she can articulate. At times the walls of the dormitory seem to be thinning out; lying in her cot in the middle of the night, Esther believes she can see through the floors above her into the night sky.

And one winter afternoon when the house seems particularly quiet, the toddlers napping, the older girls doing laundry in the garden, more than nine years since her first generalized seizure, Esther hears a steam engine roar to life in the distance. She stops in the hall at the top of the stairs and clenches her eyes.

"No," she whispers.

It roars toward her. Hirschfeld House vanishes; Esther walks through a lightless city at nightfall. Between the buildings are warrens and featureless alleys and stony burrows. Soot rains from the sky. Every doorway she passes is crammed with dirty, silent people. They sip gray broth or squat on their heels or study the lines of their hands. Crows flap from gutters. Leaves fly along the streets and die and rise into the air once more.

A boy passes her dragging a sledge piled with ragged coats and broken canes and unidentifiable junk. "Where are you going?" Esther asks him, and tugs his sleeve, and he turns to her and sleet drips from his hair into his eyes and he coughs into his hand and does not reply.

Esther wakes at the bottom of the stairs with a bone sticking out of her wrist.

11

These things she sees—seething crowds, processions through the snow, a man and a woman in an unfurnished house—they are no more real than the subjects of her drawings. Right? They are dreams, fantasies, tricks of neurochemistry. They are landscapes of the imagination. This is what the doctors insist; this is what anyone rational would believe. To contemplate that they might be otherwise would be to do violence to a person's common sense.

And yet why then does eighty-one-year-old Esther, in her clearest moments, begin trying to sneak out of the clinic? Why—seemingly every times she blinks—do flashes of her childhood friends flow across the undersides of her eyelids? She watches Hanelore peer out windows, Miriam walk down broken streets, Inga go to sleep in front of a cold hearth. The toddlers stay toddlers. The teenagers stay teenagers. Esther thinks: By staying alive I am keeping them from ceasing to exist entirely. Or else I'm holding them in a borderland against their will.

Twice she is caught by nurses as she limps past their station in her gown in the night, barefoot, trailing an IV tube. They put her back in her bed. They telephone Robert. Orderlies clatter past. Somewhere a toilet flushes. How much longer can she listen to this monstrous, mechanical, pounding thrum?

By her eighth day in the clinic Robert is practically crying as soon as she starts in on him. Urgency glows in her face; Robert winces in the corner chair and folds himself over his knees.

"Robert," Esther says. "Please." Out the window the clouds have darkened considerably. "Do I look like I have a lot of time left?"

His voice quivers. "You're asking me to help you die, Grandmom."

"No. No. I'm asking you to help me live."

He takes her out of the clinic in the middle of a thunderstorm. The nurses are gathered at a window to watch the rain, and Robert and Esther make straight for the elevator. They ride six flights down and walk out the sliding front doors. Rain assaults the parking lot. They sit in the Nissan and run the heater; the windshield wipers fly back and forth.

He whispers to himself as he drives. Taillights slug forward along the interstate. Esther leans her head against the headrest. Her left side buzzes with a curious numbness. The far edges of the highway seem to glow; headlights ripple in the rain. Esther closes her eyes; she sees the blush in Bela Cohn's cheeks from warm bathwater, all her blood vessels open. She sees the egg-shaped face of two-year-old Anita Weiss turn up to her, eyes shining. She sees the forehead of Regina Goldschmidt bunch into furrows, threatening to tell Frau

Cohen about some transgression or another. She sees the quick, busy hands of Hanelore Goldschmidt, and the dark, wild beauty of Miriam Ingrid Bergen. She sees Hamburg in the months before they left it: the blacked-out windows, the gloom of Laufgraben and Beneckestrasse, the sense that the city had become a twilit labyrinth, as if the trisecting realities of her life, her drawings, and her seizures had all fused into one.

Rain pounds the windshield. The air smells like iron. "Thank you," whispers Esther. "Thank you, Robert."

12

The police condemn a Jewish nursing home four blocks away, and Frau Cohen takes in twenty of its elderly residents. The men crowd into the parlor; the women divide themselves between the sewing room and the dormitories. Two weeks later ten more elderly people appear at the front door. By mid-January, Number 30 Papendam brims with noise, anxiety, and lice. Every Wednesday Frau Cohen boils pots of disinfectant. Displaced people are camped out in the cellar, in the custodian's closet, in the classroom, and on the floor of the dining room—a typist, a former librarian, a retired professor, a rug merchant, a jeweler. Each walls off a few square feet of floor space with suitcases, some fractured polygon in which to lay out clothes or play cards or dream.

Miriam and Esther drag their cots up to the Hirschfeld House attic: a refuge strung with cobwebs and crammed with ancient donations. Twin hexagonal windows look out over the neighboring rooftops. With the windows open they can hear the snuffling of the confined people in the houses around them, whispered prayers rising through ceilings, rumors drifting along hallways, final hopes settling into walls.

In the back of the attic looms a half-ton cedar wardrobe, thick-paneled, painted white. Esther can stand on the low shelf inside without her head reaching the top. She starts spending whole afternoons up there, clambering over the old tables and lamps to kneel in the huge wardrobe and draw labyrinths with the stub of her last pencil onto the smooth, white interior panels. She draws bridges interlacing above other bridges, column-faced temples, trees growing upside-down in caverns. As if inventing a haven into which she and Miriam might flee.

It's March when Esther descends into the dining room and sees Dr. Rosenbaum talking with Frau Cohen. He's wearing a brown suit and a maroon tie and at first glance Esther decides he must not be real.

But he is. He's frighteningly thin. The hems of his trousers are pulped and one shoe is missing a lace. Half-moons of dirt are grooved under his fingernails. He embraces Esther for a long time. From a pocket he withdraws two pencils, brand new, bright red. To Esther their very existence seems almost impossible.

She whispers in his ear. "I ran out of medicine."

"Everybody has run out of everything."

"And I've been seeing people crammed into houses. People squatting on sidewalks. Waiting for something."

Dr. Rosenbaum nods. "Like when you were little."

"There are more of them now," Esther says.

He was in a labor camp for nearly a year. They only released him, he says, because he is a doctor. He has not seen his wife since he was taken away. "Minsk," he mumbles. "They say they sent her to Minsk."

Dr. Rosenbaum spends nearly all his time at Number 30 Papendam, examining the sick, plucking nits from the children's heads, or sitting in the garden, oblivious to the cold, collar unbuttoned, coat around his shoulders, his back against a tree, his big hands in his lap like listless machines. At night he goes to sleep among the men, his grizzled head laid across his instrument bag, his steel-framed glasses folded atop his chest. Esther sits with him whenever she can. "Minsk," she whispers. "Do you think she's happy there?"

"Happy?" asks Dr. Rosenbaum. He looks down at Esther with a look she cannot understand—it seems part heartache, part wistfulness, part amazement. He pats her head and looks away.

The days ratchet past. Frau Cohen drills her charges in ever-increasing regimentation—reading requirements, calculation speeds, Bible stories. Homework, supper, prayer, sleep. But for Esther time is beginning to disintegrate; twice in April she finds herself a block away and cannot remember how she got there. Sometimes she finds Miriam is holding her hand in the attic, or on a bench outside an unfamiliar house.

"You wandered off, Esther. You wouldn't listen to me. You kept asking me where you were."

She rests her head on Miriam's chest; she listens to her friend's slow, reliable breathing.

Years earlier, in what seems now like a former world, Dr. Rosenbaum had taken several of the girls to the cinema for Esther's birthday. The newsreel before the film showed a temple in Paris. Inside, beneath a huge, vaulted dome, a big, golden ball swung from a two-hundred-foot wire. On the bottom of the ball was a pin, and as it swung the pin scraped a design into sand scattered across the floor. Foucault's pendulum marked the turning of the Earth, said the narrator; it always swung; it never stopped.

Now, sitting with her ear against Miriam's rib cage, Esther can see the pendulum swinging above the city: huge, terrible, swinging on and on, ruthless, incessant; it grooves and regrooves its inhuman truth into the air.

13

In Ohio Robert makes his grandmother meals, telephones his parents twice daily, and sleeps on Esther's sofa. Occasionally he opens his notebook, intending to work on his thesis, and sketches in the margins.

Esther seems happier, he thinks, to be at home, among her houseplants and drawings and teakettles. She can get herself dressed; with a cane she can move in a slow triangle from the bathroom to the bedroom to the kitchen. In two weeks his parents will be home; in a month Robert will be back at school.

Two days after returning from the clinic Esther is standing at her bathroom sink when the train roars in the distance. She takes a knee, then lets herself down onto the carpet. In something like a dream she watches Miriam, Hanelore, and five-year-old Ilouka Croner walk ruined, buckled streets. Gulls cruise overhead like ghosts. They pass the rusting skeleton of a crane and listen to a roof leak into a hollow warehouse and wander through factories stripped of machinery. Finally they reach the twenty-story building Miriam has been looking for. When the girls look up they can see a grid of windows narrowing as they rise and the naked struts of the huge radio antenna pointing into the sky. Its beacon flashes green, goes dark, flashes again.

The stairwell is unlocked and unlit. Hanelore leads; Miriam carries Ilouka on her shoulders. Fifteen flights, sixteen flights. At the top floor is a single door with no knob. Hanelore looks back at Miriam, then pushes it open. The entire top story is an expansive square room with no dividing walls. Six windows on each side look down onto a panorama of the city.

The girls step inside, breathing heavily. In the center of the room a chrome broadcast microphone sits in a stand on top of a wooden table. No wires lead from the microphone. There appears to be no other entrance into the space. Just twenty-four windows, several missing their glass. And the table. And the microphone on top.

Miriam sets Ilouka down. The harbor beyond the city is calm and gray beneath a slow drizzle. Along its shoreline strands of weed are strung. A fallen promenade has slumped off its piers. Fields of rain fall across the water. A low, wet breeze flies through the broken windows.

No boats winking out there. No buoys sounding their bells. Nothing on the horizon.

Rain falls on the sea. Out there fish travel in numberless schools and whales freight their colossal hearts through the cold dark. Ilouka looks up at Hanelore. "What is that?"

"It's a microphone."

"What's it for?"

"For talking to people."

"What people?"

Hanelore looks at Miriam. Miriam walks barefoot to the table in her ragged dress. She leans over the microphone. She whispers, "Esther?"

14

"I saw Frau Rosenbaum," Esther tells Dr. Rosenbaum. He is sitting in his usual place against the tree in the garden. It's a bright spring day and several of the people working among the seedlings straighten and look over. "I saw her walking through a city. She was singing to herself."

Frau Cohen is washing pots in the corner of the yard. "You should be in arithmetic, Esther," she says.

Esther says, "She sang, *What can grow, grow without rain? What can burn and never end?*"

Dr. Rosenbaum sits up very straight. He looks at Esther with his palms pressed flat against the ground.

"That's enough, Esther," says Frau Cohen. To Dr. Rosenbaum she says, "She doesn't know what she's saying."

"They were in a city but they walked out of the city and through a forest into a valley full of tents. They were all moving toward these tents and the fabric of the tents was flapping in the wind. Frau Rosenbaum sang, *A stone, a stone can grow, grow without rain; Love, love can burn and never end.*"

Emotions are flowing across Dr. Rosenbaum's face like clouds; he is, Esther realizes, clutching her forearm.

"Enough, Esther!" says Frau Cohen.

"Draw it for me," whispers Dr. Rosenbaum.

She draws the scene as she remembers it on the interior of the doors of the white wardrobe with her last pencil. She draws a sprawling, smoking city with a harbor on one side and a forest on the other. At the far edge of the forest she draws hundreds of tents hemmed in by the walls of a valley.

Finally she draws Frau Rosenbaum, a tiny figure in a long procession of pilgrims: silver hair, a long coat, her mouth open in song.

After three days Esther calls Dr. Rosenbaum into the attic. He climbs into the wardrobe, knees cracking. With a candle in his fist he studies the drawings; he moves his face closer; he mutters to himself.

Esther sits on the floor on her hands. The old doctor hunkers in the wardrobe, back to her, the candlelight silhouetting him. After a minute she sees him extend a long finger and lightly touch the figure of his wife amidst the inch-high rows of pilgrims.

She thinks: And when the last one of them dies, we finally die our third death.

When the doctor climbs out of the wardrobe, he looks at Esther for a very long time. In the morning he's gone.

15

In Ohio seizures flow through Esther. A steady electrochemical pulsing washes up out of her temporal lobe and overtakes the coordinated firing of her consciousness. Her arms stiffen, her head falls back. The seizures no longer seem to impair her consciousness so much as amplify it. Through her right eye she can see Robert turn her on her side and hold her hand; through her left the backyard diminishes gradually: first the trees, then the grass, then the sky, until all that remains are the posts of the garden fence, like bolts of white cloth, housedresses rippling against the encroaching gray.

Maybe, she tells Robert, during her clearest moments, a person can experience an illness as a kind of health. Maybe not every disease is a deficit, a taking away. Maybe what's happening to her is an opening, a window, a migration. Maybe that's what Dr. Rosenbaum saw in her; maybe that's what he was thinking as he stared into the white wardrobe that afternoon up in the attic of Number 30 Papendam: that there was something in her worth saving. Maybe she'd lived these past sixty-five years to serve as a conduit between her memories and Robert's, to hold the girls in place long enough so that he, too, could hear an echo of their voices as they washed through the trees.

"Get your recorder," she tells her grandson.

Robert nods uneasily. He brings her soup; he brings her triangles of toast. He tells his parents Esther is doing better. He tells them she is as indestructible as ever.

In seizures Esther watches Miriam walk the girls in groups through the abandoned city to the tall building with the radio mast on its roof. The girls look up at the flashing beacon at the very top and then they climb the long flights to the twentieth floor. Their voices come to Esther in the bathroom, in bed, on the deck in full daylight. She sits very quietly; the leaves rustle; she hears the faintest scratch of a girl's voice, riding along beneath the breeze. She hears a little girl say, "But it's not even hooked up."

"I'll go," a third voice says, suddenly amplified. "Papa worked in a furniture store. We lit candles on Fridays, kept the Sabbath. Even after I was sent to Hirschfeld House I thought everybody did the same. It wasn't until I saw the signs and asked Frau Cohen what they meant that I knew we were Jewish."

Or: "Okay. Right. I had an uncle in the United States. When I was thirteen—this was years after my parents were gone—Frau Cohen wrote him a letter asking if he could sponsor a trip. For me. Whether he could find me a place to live, feed me, all that. Get me out of Hamburg. I told her not to write that he'd have to feed me. I told her to tell him I could find my own food. My uncle wrote back right away. *Things are tight here*, he wrote."

A long pause. Esther closes her eyes. She hears the voice say, "He didn't know."

Sometimes she sees the girls above her garden. They trudge up a long, switchbacked staircase, the youngest holding the hands of the oldest; they sit up on the twentieth floor in the big square room, a quarter mile above Esther's yard, taking their turns at the microphone, some of them lying down with their hands laced behind their heads, listening to the harbor wind streak through the broken windows, a hundred feet above the treetops.

Esther whispers their names into the darkness of the backyard. Ellen, Bela, Regina, Hanelore, Anita, Zita, Inga, Gerda, Else, Miriam. Robert is at her elbow. His recorder is in her lap. "Tell me about them, Grandmom."

"Anita Weiss had a lisp. She used to catch her tongue between her teeth. Zita could never keep the hair out of her eyes. Regina had a widow's peak. The other girls said she was mean but I think she was always afraid. She didn't trust that anything could be permanent."

"Who was your best friend?"

"Miriam," Esther murmurs. "I loved her. She was older than me. Just a few years younger than you are now."

Robert hands her a mug of tea. A minute passes, or an hour. Why, Esther wonders, do any of us believe our lives lead outward through time? How do we know we aren't continually traveling inward, toward our centers? Because this is how it feels to Esther when she sits on her deck in Geneva, Ohio, in the last spring of her life; it feels as if she is being drawn down some path that leads deeper inside, toward a miniature, shrouded, final kingdom that has waited within her all along.

Robert's parents call from China. They need a certain lawyer's phone number; they need Robert to deliver something to his father's office. They plan to be home by the fifth of July. They want to know if Robert needs them home sooner.

"It's not awful," says Robert. "Being with her. It's amazing, actually." He is quiet awhile; his mother breathes on the other end. "But I don't know how much longer I can do it."

That afternoon he pulls a two-wheeled bike trailer made for children from the depths of his parents' garage. He straps seat cushions inside, mounts it behind his bicycle; in the evening he helps Esther into the trailer and tows her down their long street.

They go slowly; he avoids traffic and hills. That night they ride for a full hour, through the dusk and into the moonlight, passing farms and occasional subdivisions, down the long, flat, rural roads of northeastern Ohio, maybe one car passing every ten minutes, and Esther feels as if she is being pedaled through a half-world of shimmering trees and fields and water towers and great flexing pools of shadow. In the distance, over Lake Erie, hazy thunderheads stack up in coral-colored towers. Robert pedals hard and with great seriousness, and Esther feels the blood pumping through her.

“Are you comfortable, Grandmom?” Robert asks, turning around, panting.

“More than you know,” Esther says.

16

On July 26, four hundred and three English aircraft bomb Hamburg at midnight. Miriam and Esther watch from the attic windows. Spotlights spring up from points around the harbor. Hundreds of filaments of red light ascend from hidden gun emplacements. At their apexes the threads bloom into ganglia of red flak, white in their centers.

From their dormer windows the girls watch incendiaries fall through rooftops twenty blocks away and their casings open into light. White, phosphoric flames flow like water into gutters. Within seconds independent fires have linked up; soon entire houses are in flames. Above them clouds of smoke and ash bloom in harlequin colors: red, green, orange. Whole quarters of sky flare, then are sucked back into darkness. It feels to Esther as if she is staring up into a vast, electric brain. And from the brain little flaming sheets of paper and pillows and books and shingles rain slowly down over the city.

Two days later the summons finally arrives for the Hirschfeld girls. The eagle and the cross on a thick envelope. No stamp. As if delivered from the office of God. Frau Cohen calls the girls from their various chores; they sit facing her while she unfolds her reading glasses.

Around them a thousand houses in Hamburg smolder. Around them prisoners of war load bodies onto wagons and sailors drowse over their guns. In the garden behind the orphanage a former bank manager rakes between rows of cabbages.

They are to travel on foot to a school gymnasium beside the Central Hotel. From there a deportation agent will escort them to the Ludwigslust railway station. There are long, meticulous lists of what it is advisable to bring—nightdresses, mittens, candles, shoe polish, eyeglasses—and what is not advisable—rugs, plants, books, matches. There are directions for how everything should be labeled and conveyed; each girl is given a deportation number.

Where, where, where? Regina Goldschmidt finally gets the question out first. The girls lean closer to hear the reply; several clamp their hands over their hearts. Frau Cohen flips through the papers.

"Warsaw."

Esther tries to catch her breath. She has the sense that if she lets herself blink, she will see another world beneath this one. Warsaw—how many times has she imagined Nancy Schwartzenberger's life there? She tries to remember Frau Rosenbaum's picture postcards. Old town. Wilanów Palace. The Vistula River.

All afternoon the girls pack their things. Esther concentrates—candles, shoe polish, nightdress, arithmetic book. Underwear, birth certificate, thread. She thinks of Nancy Schwartzenberger sewing buttons. How old will Nancy be now? How exciting if they can manage to meet up with her!

Maybe, Esther decides, they will have more space in Warsaw. Maybe there will be apothecaries with white gloves and loaded shelves.

Auswanderung. The paths of the birds.

At the other end of the attic, nine-year-old Hanelore Goldschmidt besieges Miriam with questions: Will there be school? What about gymnastics? What kind of animals will they have? Will we be allowed to go to the zoo? Miriam goes downstairs, helps Hanelore choose among her few possessions. Before supper the girls carry their suitcases to the front door and leave them in a row with their tags bristling from the handles, all of it to be brought in wheelbarrows to the station in the morning.

After prayers Esther and Miriam climb the staircase to the attic and push open the trapdoor. They lie down beside the big white wardrobe. The attic beams tick in the heat; spiders draw their webs between rafters.

"Warsaw can't be worse than this," Esther says.

Miriam says nothing.

"Don't you think so?"

Miriam rolls onto her side. "The only thing I've learned so far, Esther," she says, "is that things can always get worse."

Beside her friend in the attic that night, Esther slips into dreams. When she comes back into herself it is very late. Not a single light shines out the window. Someone is walking hunched through the furniture around her. The figure stoops in front of the girls' cots for a long moment. Watery breathing. Cracking knees. Miriam sleeps.

"Dr. Rosenbaum?" He looks thinner than ever in the gloom of the attic.

"Very quiet," he whispers.

"What's happening?"

"Shhh."

She thinks: He came to say goodbye. In the morning we're leaving, so he came to say goodbye to me.

"Your dress," he says. "The coat, too."

She pulls on stockings, laces her shoes. Miriam does not stir. Esther follows Dr. Rosenbaum down five flights of stairs, past sleeping children and muttering crones and doomed men, at last into the parlor, where he peers with all his attention through a gap in the curtains. Someone snores at the other end of the room. Someone else coughs.

Are they leaving so early? Why not wait until morning? Every time she tries to ask him something, he hushes her. Out in the street the springs of a truck ring dully as its tires rattle across the cobbles. "The curfew—" Esther says, and Dr. Rosenbaum hisses, "Now," and hurries her out of the house and through the gate. The truck's headlights are not running and Papendam is very dark. The truck's back swings open; inside is a void, a blankness out of which scared faces slowly bloom: the truckbed is stuffed with people.

"Hurry," says Dr. Rosenbaum.

"But Miriam!" cries Esther. "My bag!"

"Go!" says Dr. Rosenbaum, and pushes her in.

17

Eleven murdered girls wake up on the floor of a tall, unremarkable row house. Esther wakes in her bed in Ohio, her grandson asleep down the hall on the couch. Frau Cohen wakes at Number 30 Papendam in 1942, washes her face, and pulls on her cleanest housedress. She laces her shoes, pauses on the threshold of the kitchen, and sends up her requests to God. Please watch over us as we begin our journey. Please don't let me falter.

Within the wet enclosure of a single mind a person can fly from one decade to the next, one country to another, past to present, memory to imagination. Esther wakes again, this time in a cottage in the woods. The ceiling is low and the furniture is rough-hewn. Old pickaxes and sawblades and crampons are fixed haphazardly to the walls—the effect is of a rusting, historical suffocation. The cupboards are dens of superstition: filled with a putrescent reek, jars of dark elixirs, unlabeled pain remedies, molasses, crystals, something marked *belladonna*, something marked *trumpet of death*. Out the tiny windows hundreds of birch trunks gleam bone white against the dawn. A home to forest people involved in some dark, gnomish magic.

Birds flit here and there. In front of the cottage Dr. Rosenbaum is asleep on a log bench without a blanket to cover him. She fears he is dead but when she says his name he opens his eyes.

"What happened?"

"You seized. We brought you here."

"I don't remember."

Birds flit here and there, crying thinly. The sky is colorless.

"I should be with *them*," Esther whispers.

"You're tired," Dr. Rosenbaum says. "This has been an ordeal." As if this were it, as if now it were over. Esther hears herself whisper to Miriam, years before, in the darkness of the dormitory: *I hope we are sent together.*

Dr. Rosenbaum smiles at her. "It's best to stay inside."

She spends the day washing in and out of shallow nightmares. Dr. Rosenbaum boils a pot of turnips; he sits with her and holds her hand. In the evening he hands her a letter handwritten in English, a sheaf of British pounds, and an address in London.

"When the truck comes back," he says, "I'll return to Hamburg."

Esther's vision swims with fear. "No. Please. Miriam. And the others."

Dr. Rosenbaum squeezes her hand between his two big, cold palms. "Where they are going, you do not want to go."

Esther tries to compose a sensible protest. She thinks of the man and woman sitting cross-legged on the floor, staring out at snow; she thinks of the druggist who slit his own throat. She thinks of the thousands of people squatting in doorways: starving, dirty, waiting.

"Go live your life, Esther." A half-hour later he's gone. She is picked up that night by a man with six other children riding in a trailer beneath a sheet of canvas; they ride together through the dawn. A boy whispers that they have entered Denmark; another argues that they are going to Belgium. One of them has wet himself and soon their rocking, lightless compartment reeks of urine. At midmorning the man hides them in a windowless, dirt-floored, seven-by-seven cellar.

They spend the next thirty-six hours there, a girl's hip pressed into Esther's shoulder, a young boy sniffling against her other side, the yelps of faraway dogs and the long silences of nightfall and the rumbles of airplanes passing far above. Rumors ripple through the children: they are being sent to Ireland, or England, or South America. A boy repeats, "We are going somewhere better," over and over, as if saying it will make it so. Once a day someone unlocks the door and pitches in a loaf of hard, dark bread. Then the door is locked again.

All through that time Esther's face is crammed up against a board and in the board is a large, dark knot. She stares into that knot and sweats into her nicest dress until there is no longer any water in her to sweat out. Over and over the words pass through Esther's mind: *I should be with them.* She watches the Hirschfeld girls climb the stairs of a glowing palace in Warsaw. She watches the doors open; the girls step into a white foyer. They stare up into the thousand glittering diamonds of a chandelier. Someone in uniform comes down a long staircase to greet them. The doors slowly close. The light fades.

The cellar smells of sweat, hunger, terror, and human waste. The others know no more and no less. Whenever there is enough light Esther stares into the knot of wood until its grains squirm with miniscule figures, carriages and trams, streetlamps and little coachmen dressed in velvet carrying whips, weathered houses and naked trees, and as she stares into it she realizes it contains a dark city, alive, microscopic, teeming with people and rain and grime.

Twice Esther has grand mal seizures down there in the darkness. Her legs rattle against the slatted walls as the others try to hold her still, someone's hand clamped over her mouth, someone else holding her on her side. She sees Miriam Ingrid Bergen riding a train, peering out a window, one of the younger girls in her lap. She sees a crowd of thousands waiting out in the darkness. Esther comes to and hunches over her knees, feeling as if her mind is tearing itself apart. She thinks: I never want to have another seizure again.

After the fourth day the children are smuggled to London onboard a fishing boat with guns newly welded to its bow. In Anglia, Esther shows a longshoreman her money and the letter from Dr. Rosenbaum. She is taken to a clinic where a man in a doctor's coat gives her a set of secondhand clothes, a bottle of phenobarbital, and emigration papers for the United States.

18

Inga Hoffman says, "There was a Jewish shoe store on Benderstrasse. The night they were smashing all the windows we watched a boy break in and crawl inside. His father was waiting on the street and when the boy came out with four pairs of shoes he looked down at the boy and scolded him. I thought he was scolding him for stealing but he was scolding him because one of the pairs he had taken had two right shoes. He sent the boy back in to correct the problem." She tries a laugh but it comes across closer to a gasp.

Little Zita Dettmann says, "Not everyone was mean to us. Two ladies left a crate of pastries on the front steps. Do you remember that? I put one in my mouth right away. Inside was strawberry jam. Strawberry jam!"

An even smaller voice sings, *One little goat, one little goat, which my father bought for two zuzim…*

Gerda Kopf says, "You hear stuff like your whole life passes in front of your eyes. But it's not true. A life is really big, it contains a billion things, as many needles as there are on a pine tree. There's no music, but there is a sound—like a far-off screech. Or smoke rising. Or like a woman inhaling a little, like she's about to sing."

A pause. A shuffling. Esther sits on the backyard deck and rain thrums on the umbrella Robert has braced over her. A sweetness rises in the air, rich, intertwining—hollyhock, rain on grass. Esther hears

Regina Goldschmidt's voice wash through the trees. "The lady at the end of the block had no home. Everyone called her Mrs. Glasses. She slept on the sidewalk for years. The other girls would say: Why doesn't she just leave? I knew why. Mrs. Glasses had nobody. She had given up. I brought her a hairbrush because her hair was disgusting. And then I got to thinking she was cold and so I gave her my red scarf, too. My brown one was nicer anyway. Then I brought her the afghan with the colored circles on it from the cupboard in Frau Cohen's room. I set it down beside Mrs. Glasses while she was sleeping. Her hands were scaly, I remember, and I was glad she didn't wake up. Two days later the police took her away for stealing and I didn't say anything. I never saw Mrs. Glasses again. None of us did. That's my memory. That's what I remember."

The rain slows. The leaves drip. The garden steams.

19

The Jewish Rescue Authority places Esther with a childless couple in New Jersey coincidentally named the Rosenbaums. They are first-generation Romanian immigrants and they live on a two-bedroom houseboat. At the tiny table in what the Rosenbaums call their galley they feed Esther meals that seem obscenely large: slabs of eggplant, hunks of chicken, steaming bowls of green-bean soup. Three times a day the three of them sit down to eat at that table, in that floating house that smells of bilgewater and foot cream and baklava.

Esther writes Miriam every day. Mr. Rosenbaum bundles the letters in groups of six and mails them from the post office in Toms River. Where they go, who they reach, what hands dispose of them, Esther will never know.

Stories of the camps trickle into the newspapers; they are all Mrs. Rosenbaum can talk about. Why? is the question Esther continually asks herself. Why did Dr. Rosenbaum save her, why was she pulled out, why not Hanelore, Regina, Else? Why not Miriam?

She swallows a steady stream of anticonvulsants. She sells tickets at the movie theater. She tries to believe that the world can be a reasonable place. But most days the silence of her cramped, chilly room on the Rosenbaums' boat overwhelms her: lit an eerie blue from a pier light outside, no voices of children, no music, only distant foghorns and ropes chiming mournfully against masts, everything rocking back and forth.

Memory becomes something to be subverted and walled off. Esther works on maintaining her attention only in the present. There is always the now—an endlessly adjusting smell of the wind, the shining of the stars, the deep five-call *chirrup chirrup* of the cicadas in the park. There is the now that is today falling into the now that is tonight: dusk on the rim of the Atlantic, the flicker of the movie screen, a submergence of history, a tanker cleaving imperceptibly across the horizon.

It is never warm enough. She buys spring dresses and quilted jackets and walks to the theater on a hot day but feels some deep chill within her. But she does not seize; she does not see the man and woman peering out into the snow; she does not have to confront ragged, swelling crowds crammed into row houses, or the unutterable prospect of finding her friends' faces among them.

Esther is twenty-six and fluent in English when she meets the boy who will become her husband. He is small and gregarious and perpetually on the brink of loud and catching laughter. He meets her at the movie theater. He is a hospital orderly but wants to be a bicyclist; he dreams of opening a bicycle shop; he sits her down on park benches and tells her about his plans. They'll go somewhere far away, they'll sell bikes, they'll have a family.

The contents of his plans are not nearly as important to Esther as their sound—the deep sureness of them. He is so young! It amazes her, after the war, that the world can still make young people. And his voice—he has a voice like a piece of silk you might remove from a drawer only very occasionally, something you'd want to run your hands over again and again.

That she can be alive with this boy—share vanilla ice cream; stroll through markets, buy cabbages big as cannonballs—sometimes fills Esther with a paralyzing, breathtaking shame.

And yet isn't there a blessedness, too? Isn't she beginning to breathe again, the way an animal might breathe after running from a predator for a long time, and finally slowing, and looking up, and watching the leaves wave overhead in their multitudes? She was alive, she was still alive. She could lay her head on this boy's chest and listen to the tumble of his heartbeat. She could stare at the crystal doorknob of her tiny ticket-taker's booth for an entire afternoon, a pad of drawing paper in her lap, waiting for the evening sunlight to come through the left-hand window at the proper angle. When it finally does it sprays prisms of color across the wall.

She and the boyfriend move to Ohio. They get married; they get a loan; they start his bicycle shop. Everything is round: rims, tires, sprockets, chain loops. Everything smells of chain grease; everyone pays in cash. Esther works the cash register or opens her sketchpad on the glass counter and draws while her husband fiddles with a series of portable radios, a spectrum of American stations: country, jazz, folk, swing.

The arch of a handlebar, sweeping back to the grips. Thirty spoked wheels hanging from hooks. Freewheels and hubs, chain stays and cranks; the concentric spirals of painted chain guards. Round-headed screws gleaming in pails. Bearings in jars, bearings in buckets. Sheaves of spokes tied with strips of cloth. A rack of bells: chrome, brass, aluminum.

They have a son. After school he draws beside his mother at the counter, the two of them working on matching sheets of paper, and when he gets older he works beside his father, running the links of a salvaged bicycle chain back and forth through a basin of oil, watching the rust fall away, feeling the rivets ride cleanly in their bushings, lubricant beading in the little golden hairs on his wrists.

Out, away, *Auswanderung*. Esther builds for herself as modest and normal and steady a life as she can manage. She is not allowed to drive a car; her medication continues to give her upset stomachs. Occasionally she is seized with wild, clutching feelings of dread. She reaches for her husband's shape in the night; she clings to him.

Sometimes Esther stares at the small row of medications along the kitchen windowsill—an endlessly rotating series of bottles—and thinks: I could stop. I could go back. But then her son walks in looking for a snack, or the telephone rings, or she steps over to her drawing table and goes back to work.

Mrs. Rosenbaum, still living on her houseboat in New Jersey, is the one who sends the deportation manifest. Esther is thirty-five years old when it arrives; it waits in the mailbox between a utility bill and an advertising flyer. Inside the first envelope is a second, and Esther waits two days to open it. By then she has decided that she knows what it will say.

She thinks: The others will be there but maybe Miriam will not. How could Miriam die? Miriam was never a person with illusions; she always had the strength of her own pragmatism. Maybe only the deluded had been slaughtered. But of course everyone was slaughtered.

Forty cards. Several of them have hundreds of names on them.

It is easy enough to find July 29, 1942. Twelve birthdates, twelve girls. Miriam's name among them. Esther's too.

20

Robert's voice grows fainter, as if Esther is receding behind him, as if he were still pulling her behind his bicycle and now the trailer has uncoupled. Finally all Esther can hear as she sits on her deck on the last day of her life is Miriam's voice. The backyard is gray at every hour; Robert is little more than a warm presence.

"At the edge of the city we found a forest," Miriam's voice says, "and we'll have to go all the way through the forest. And then at the end we'll climb a hill and when we reach the top, down below is mist, Esther, a thick ribbon of it, hiding the view. The vapors fall and condense and whirl around themselves. But sometimes they part for a moment, and down there in that valley I saw a thousand tents, Esther, ten thousand maybe, each with a lamp burning inside it, all of them rustling and flapping in a breeze. A whole city of golden tents glowing down there beneath the mist."

There is a pause. Then: "We're going there, Esther. You and me. All of us."

21

At dusk on the fourth of July the woods echo with the explosions of neighbors' fireworks. Robert nails a Catherine wheel to a tree and it sprays rainbows out into the night.

Esther sits on the deck with a blanket around her legs and a dreamy, lost expression on her face. Whenever Robert asks if she is uncomfortable it takes her a little while to reply that she is fine. At this very moment his parents are thirty thousand feet above the Pacific, two little girls asleep in the seats between them.

The wheel spews a last paroxysm of sparks. The darkness reasserts itself. Robert clicks on a flashlight and rummages through his box for another firework. Fireflies float and flash in the trees.

"What about one more, Grandmom? We've got tons of these."

Esther doesn't reply. Robert says, "Okay, let's do a big one." He sets his lighter to a wick and the wick burns down and a rocket fizzes into the sky.

Esther's gaze casts up through the leaves, a sea of them shifting against a flower of noiseless, golden sparks. Which part of them is her, and which part is the rest of the world? She tips backward onto the lawn. The sparks fall through the sky. A locomotive stampedes through her head.

When Esther wakes, it's night. She can feel the sanded planks of a floor beneath her knees, a windowsill beneath her fingernails. Out the window, clouds blow past stars. The more Esther looks, the more stars she sees.

Somewhere below her a little girl's voice is calling hello. Esther feels her way to the doorway. It is pitch dark in the hall. She finds a stairwell, a wobbling banister. One flight, two flights. There's a bit more light on the first floor, starlight washing through curtainless windows.

No furniture. No doors on the cupboards. Again she hears a voice, calling from somewhere outside. Esther finds the front door. Beyond is a harbor wind, and a sky swarming with infinitesimal lights.

Standing in the belt-high thistles are eleven girls, their faces smears of white in the darkness. Miriam is easy to spot: the tallest of them. Barefoot. Regal in her tattered dress. She takes Esther by the hand and helps her climb down out of the doorway. "We've been waiting," Miriam says, and smiles a sweet-faced smile. Esther breathes. The wind settles. The twelve of them stand in the thistles looking back for a moment at the empty house crouched there in the night. Then they all start walking down the street.

22

Robert is a senior in college; he's home for Thanksgiving. Five days, seven inches of snow, twenty degrees. It's the first snowfall of the year and everything is familiar and new all at once: the leafless hardwoods ringing his parents' house; the mingling smells of slush, gasoline, and firewood in the garage; the confused, wondrous looks on the faces of his two four-year-old sisters as they look out the living room windows into snow for the first time.

His father slices carrots in the kitchen. His mother wrestles the girls into matching pink snowsuits. Out the windows everything is either gray or white. The radio burbles out another storm warning; the twins stand very still as their mother pushes mittens over their hands.

Robert leads them out through the garage. A last few snowflakes slip down from the clouds. The girls plod through Robert's tracks in tandem, heads down, into the big, white amphitheater of the backyard. Soon the girls' exuberance surges; they run out in front of Robert; they laugh, fall down, roll over, and squeal. Robert lopes after them, hands in his pockets.

After a few minutes the girls trudge between the naked willows at the left edge of the yard and disappear into what was once Esther's property. Now it's vacant, a realty sign covered with snow at the end of her driveway.

Every tree, every post of the garden fence, is a candle to a memory, and each of those memories, as it rises out of the snow, is linked to a dozen more. Over there is the birdfeeder Robert broke his wrist trying to hang; over there Esther helped him bury his parakeet named Marbles. He used to throw a football onto the section of the roof above that garage window and wait for it to come rolling off the gutter. He shot a squirrel out of that locust tree and carried its body on the blade of a shovel to the compost pile. He made tie-dye T-shirts one summer day with his grandmother in the same spot where his sisters' little boot prints now crisscross the snow.

Robert's advisor has urged him to read more: armies and treaties, Roosevelt and Churchill. A proper thesis, his advisor says, will set his grandmother's life into the broader context of history. But in the end all Robert wants to do is listen to the recordings he made of Esther in the last days of her life.

Ellen, Bela, Inga, Gerda, Else, Miriam. Lately Robert foresees a different sort of project. He'll draw portraits of the girls' silhouettes, charcoal on paper, life-size, twelve shadows rendered as vividly and carefully as he can present them, some running, some sitting, some dancing, some wondering, the deportation manifest hung above them all. The point will not be to make the outlines perfectly accurate, or to set things within their proper context. The point will be to offer a sense of the shapes those girls embodied in this world. Of the women they might have been.

Anita Weiss had a lisp. Hanelore loved animals. Zita could never keep the hair out of her eyes. Regina had a widow's peak.

The twins are throwing snow up into the air and watching it glitter as it sifts down around them. One yells, "You are, you are!" and takes a few running steps and then falls onto her hands and knees. Robert helps her up. Already the heat from her face has melted the snow on it. "You're okay," he says.

Every hour, Robert thinks, all over the globe, an infinite number of memories disappear, whole glowing atlases dragged into graves. But during that same hour children are moving about, surveying territory that seems to them entirely new. They push back the darkness; they scatter memories behind them like breadcrumbs. The world is remade.

In the five days Robert will be home his sisters will learn to say "rocks," "heavy," and "snowman." They'll learn the different smells of snow and the slick feel of a plastic sled as their brother drags them down the driveway.

We return to the places we're from; we trample faded corners and pencil in new lines. "You've grown up so fast," Robert's mother tells him at breakfast, at dinner. "Look at you." But she's wrong, thinks Robert. You bury your childhood here and there. It waits for you, all your life, to come back and dig it up.

Now the girls are clawing sticks out of the snow and tracing shapes with them. Above them the clouds shift and—abruptly—sunlight avalanches across the yard. The shadows of trees lunge across the lawn. The snow seems to incandesce. Robert has forgotten that sunlight can look so pure, pouring out of the sky, splashing across the snow. It brings tears to his eyes.

Jing-Wei, the taller of the girls, lifts a long, black branch out of the snow and tries to hand it to her brother. "For Rob-ert," she says, and blinks up at him.

TWENTY QUESTIONS

by Bridget Clerkin

When I was a kid and my mother found it in herself to cook dinner, she would get the youngest of us—me and my two younger brothers—to help. "Who will help me wash the carrots?" she'd say, like the Little Red Hen. "Who will help me set the table?"

I think of this every time Johnny starts one of his guessing games with one of the kids. It was a towheaded schoolboy from Brentwood this time. "Do you know how to play twenty questions?" Johnny asked. This was new. Usually he just made them guess things. Which hand it's in. A special number between one and fifteen.

The kid shakes his head.

"It's because of the video games nowadays," Johnny says, looking over at me. "Do you play video games?" The kid nods. "Well, forget all that. Here's how twenty questions works. If I'm the guesser, you think of something like a person or a food or a cartoon character, and I ask you a yes or no question. And only yes or no questions after that. So we start out, and you're thinking of, say, uh, Benjamin Franklin—you know who Benjamin Franklin is?"

The kid nods.

"Good," Johnny says. "So I ask if you're thinking of a person. And you say yes. And I ask if it's a boy. And you say yes. And then I ask if he's famous." Johnny nods at the boy, who jerks his head yes. "And you say yes."

"Wait," I say. "Wait. You get the animal-vegetable-mineral thing, first."

Johnny straightens up and faces me. "What?"

"You ask if it's an animal, vegetable, or mineral. It doesn't count as the first question. It's like the introduction."

"Well, Beth, I don't know what kind of bizarre, regional version y'all were playing—"

"The normal version," I say.

Johnny puts his hand on the kid's knee. The kid looks down at Johnny's hand. On the knuckles in black and red are the letters T H A T. He doesn't have anything on the other hand. He wanted his two favorite artists to do one hand each, or at least his two favorite artists whom he knew, and who would give him a discount, but he says he got in a fight after he had the right hand's knuckles done and because of what happened he can't remember the names of any of the dogs he's ever had in his life or what he was going to get on his other hand. He got hit a few times in the head with his own brass knuckles. That didn't stop him from carrying them around, though.

"So you wanna play?" Johnny asks the kid, whose name is Skylar. Johnny nods to prod him and the kid nods, too.

"Okay. Think of something."

"Spy Kids," the kid blurts out. This is maybe the third thing he's said the whole time.

"Ah, no," Johnny says. "You're not supposed to tell me. Why don't I go first?"

Skylar nods.

"Okay," Johnny says.

"Animal, vegetable, or mineral," I prompt, when the kid doesn't say anything.

"Animal, vegetable, or mineral," the kid whispers.

"Animal," Johnny says. He takes his Leatherman from his back pocket and puts it on the floor, and then he sits down Indian-style. I think he should get THIS on the other hand, so it's *this* and *that*. Say hello to *this*—left jab—and *that*—right hook. Johnny says that that's retarded. I say it's funny, but what's retarded is to let the kids see the tattoos in the first place.

The kid looks up at me. Johnny does, too.

I look at Skylar. "Is it a person?" I say. The kid says to Johnny, "Is it a person?"

Johnny says, "Yes. Yes, it is a person." He twists around and says to me, "Let the kid play. You gotta let them learn things."

I sit down next to Johnny. "Sure," I say. "Skylar, you got the hang of it?"

Skylar nods. "Is it a boy?" he says.

"It is, yes," Johnny says, proud of the kid's very first on-his-own question.

"Is he famous?"

"Yup," says Johnny. "He's on the TV right now, probably."

I want kids. We won't have blond kids like Skylar; Johnny has black hair and I have dark brown. I check the prepaid cellphone. No missed calls, which I know already because I would have heard it ring.

"Is it Benjamin Franklin?" the kid asks.

Johnny barks out a laugh. "You hear this kid?" he asks me, as if I'm not right next to him. Johnny puts his hand on my leg. "Skylar," he says, "if you try to guess every famous person you can think of, you're gonna run outta questions. You're on five right now."

"Four," I say.

"Yeah," Johnny says. "Keep going," he says to the kid.

When I was in middle school, I started to hate not just the sing-song tone of my mother's Little Red Hen thing, but also that she always asked for "help" and then stood around in the kitchen drinking or talking on the phone while whoever she had suckered in did all the work. It was always me or Jerry, who was nine, or Irving, five-ish. I was looking for little things like that to pick on, back then, to show that I hated my mother like everyone else my age hated theirs, and also like my older siblings. But I never really knew what she was getting at until later. Teaching us the value of helping people without having to be directly asked. Or letting us know that we wouldn't get any bread like the cat-dog-pig in the story, otherwise. Pure manipulation.

The first time Johnny met my mother it was Thanksgiving and I hadn't seen her in six years. My oldest sister had told me that our mother was different, by then, but that didn't mean my sister would be coming. We drove two and hours through holiday traffic from Glendora to Sunland and listened to traffic reports, Mexican talk shows, and the one CD I had in my old car—Pearl Harbor and the Explosions. She was with Paul Simonon for a time. Some people have it all. Johnny snapped the CD in half on the trip back.

By then Rita had told me about a time before Irving was born, when one day nobody responded to Mom's game. "So she peels and cooks all the fucking potatoes in the house," Rita said, "and puts them into a casserole, or something, with lots of mayo and nasty shit, as usual, and then she sits down at the table. But first she sets the whole table. And when we try to sit down to eat, she starts screaming at us. You-didn't-help. Get-away. Get-out-of-my-house."

We were sitting on the back steps and Rita was smoking. She was going through her Siouxsie Sioux stage, like most of the other upperclassmen girls. "She ate the whole fucking thing and then threw up in the kitchen sink on all the potato peelings she'd left there, and then she leaves all that there and goes out," she said. "We all wake up the next day and she's all, like, 'Who will help me clean the sink?' Which was now clogged, by the way. So here's the other thing, too. She'd used all the potatoes. We had nothing to eat. I invited myself over to my friends' houses for dinner for the rest of the week. I know Paul was ten, so you must have been about six."

I had no problem picturing my mother standing over the kitchen sink, smashing her stomach against the side of the counter. I was around fourteen or fifteen when Rita told me that story, and I didn't exactly know how to make yourself throw up, though I knew that people did it. I still don't doubt that Mom went in there and stuck her finger down her throat, or that she ate all that food because she knew it would come up.

Johnny and I got there with two pies we'd made the night before. He had made a sweet potato pie. I had made a custard pie but had forgotten to put a baking sheet under it. The spill had burned onto the bottom of our oven. At my mother's, when I went into the kitchen to put the pies in the refrigerator, the first thing she said, in that same sing-song, was, "Who will help me peel the potatoes?" Like we were still eight years old and ready to get blamed when my little brothers' dad didn't come home—not blamed for his absence, but for anything else she could notice, blamed for the fact that potatoes had skin, that the skin was still on the potatoes. Jerry and Irv, the two youngest, who were there with their wives, who had entered into perfectly normal relationships, looked at each other for a long time, then at me, and then Jerry's wife said, "I'll do it," and Jerry said, "No, let me. I'll do it, Ma."

We all eventually learned the same thing: it is a roof, it is food, but you stay away, you go out with friends, you go read at the bookstore, you get a job, you leave whoever is still in the house to pay for the dumb mistake of staying there, and you come back for the screaming fights with her and the place to sleep—and now Jerry and Irv were letting their wives fall for it. And I had fallen for it again, too. It took another hour or so for me to stand up and drag Johnny out of there, yelling all the way to the car, yelling to Johnny about her so she would hear it from the house, and yelling more, at Johnny, when I realized we had left the pies at my mother's, because you can get five cents for those pie tins at Marie Callender's. That was when Johnny popped the CD out of the player, snapped it in half, and threw it out the window. "Stop yelling. Stop being angry. Stop. And stop that fucking noise," he said out the window to the CD in the road. I hadn't even noticed it was on.

He's allowed to get angry. Not me.

But he's been patient with this kid. He's never lost his temper with any of them, even when they whine or cry or scream, and they all do. So no matter what, no matter what people say about Johnny and about me, I know he'll be a good father. And I will say to our kids, "Hey, Kid One, come here and help me with this," or "Pumpkin, time to earn your allowance. How 'bout washing those carrots for me?" or Johnny will say, "Hey, go help your mother. Do what she asks you to do." And our kids will do it and be happy.

They're on question twelve. It's a famous boy person who lives around here and is probably on the television right now and who goes to school and who is not married and who is not taller than six feet, not at all. He has blond hair. He has never been in a movie. He does not have a girlfriend. I think that's all of it so far.

Johnny rationalizes it like this. Jackie Cooper—that kid in those movies—tells a story about how a director got him to cry by taking his dog around the corner and firing shots in the air to make it seem like he was shooting the kid's dog. So when Skylar asks, "Is he dead?" and Johnny says, "Yes," and then Skylar says, "I don't know," and Johnny says, "You want a hint?" and the kid nods and Johnny says, "Okay, well, here's the hint: he's sitting right here. Do you know what being dead means? It means never seeing your parents or your friends or anything ever again," and Skylar screws his eyes up and begins to bawl, that shocked, betrayed, out-of-proportion reaction you get when a parent hits you—if you decided to look put-off by that, Johnny would tell you, "Well, hell, at least I didn't pretend to shoot a dog." But sometimes I think that a lie and a solid threat is a lot better than what the Little Red Hen did to the other barn animals, who didn't find out they were being threatened until it was too late. And really there's no reason to go the long way around when you could just straight-up yell at the kid and maybe smack him a few times.

It's on time. It's five o'clock and the prepaid cell begins to ring. I hand it to Johnny, and he answers and talks and says, "Sure, you can talk to him." The kid can barely talk he's crying so much. He tells his parents that he wants to see them. And then they get Johnny back on the line and say they want to see their kid, too.

THE ACTOR'S HOUSE

by DAVID MEANS

PASSING THE ACTOR'S HOUSE one thought of biker films, of his former edginess, of his beautiful young face on the screen, of his slight lisp—eventually a trademark of sorts—and the way he stood, slightly to one side, and tilted his head, along with the expressiveness of his features, which weren't perfect because there was something wrong in the symmetry of his face, and his nose had been broken and he tended to blink in a way that made you aware of the lens—but that didn't detract from the power of his genius, and he had three Academy Awards to his name. If you knew he lived there (when he did), you saw the house in light of his ownership. Otherwise, it was nothing more than one more grand house along the river in a long line of grand houses, and there was nothing to make it stand apart from all the others except for the wall along the front, which wasn't built by the actor but rather by the next owner, an actress and television talk-show host who found the house lacking in security and, two weeks after she moved in, began to modify it—so that, passing it at that time, one thought not only about the actor, but also about the actress, too, because from her modifications one garnered a sense of what she was like: slightly paranoid and a bit antisocial (there was a rumor afloat that some welcome-wagon soul had come to her front door with a pecan pie and had been duly told, in no uncertain terms, to fuck off). So for a few years one passed the house thinking about both souls (the actress and the actor) with a sense that, behind the walls, the actress moved about from room to room fluffing her hair with the flat of her palm, because she had a habit, most knew, of reaching up to touch her hair as if to affirm its existence—beautiful auburn hair that seemed to have as much to do with her fame as anything. But even a few years after the actor was gone, most people thought of him first and then the actress second when they passed the house, hidden behind the wall: high, built of expensive brick, with security devices in the corners on top—small red pinprick beams that couldn't be seen in normal circumstances but could be seen when it was foggy out, or at night from certain angles, coming back from the city. There were security cameras in the trees, too, and tall evergreen bushes planted just inside the wall that grew to shield the upper reaches of the house from view, so that eventually you couldn't see any of the house at all and had to look at the wall and the bushes and imagine the house as it had once been, years ago, before the talk-show host/actress and even the actor lived there and the house had been owned by the Grande Dame of the theater who had been, at least in appearance, unconcerned about privacy.

When the actor bought the house there had been a transition period in which those passing it still thought of the Grande Dame first and then the actor second (if at all), and then thought about the Grand Dame's roles on Broadway, and in several movies, and the elegance and almost Gatsbyesque essence of her personality—the splendid parties she threw over the years on soft summer nights, with sedans and chauffeurs, bored, smoking, leaning against fenders, along the curbside. But then, eventually, over time, thoughts of the Grande Dame faded and the thought of the actor came first, as the primary owner, and with his ownership a different kind of feeling, when you passed, and a sense of mystery, because he was an enigmatic actor and known just as much for his reclusive nature and strange behavior as he was for the fact that he had grown enormously fat, so that the body that had once adorned the screen, and before that the stage, was hidden beneath rings of fat, like a Russian matryoshka doll; and because he was known, too, for his ranting and his bitter anger and the high energy that seemed to reside beneath his roles in later years when, for example, in one film, he sat amid the jungle in a Buddha calm and mumbled his lines. Passing in a car, one imagined him shuffling from room to room in bedroom slippers, muttering to himself, rehearsing new roles or—in some visions—mumbling old lines that had once given life to new characters set in stone, so to speak, on the films that had recorded his gestures. Passing the actor's house one often thought of a single scene, a favorite, and remembered it while, at the same time, imagining him fat behind the walls of the house. Because many knew the house's interior—during those early days of the actor's ownership—from the tours that had been given back in the Grande Dame's days, when, once a year, she had opened her door to the general public and allowed them to traipse through, fingering the brocade bedspreads and touching her fine collection of Native American—they'd think Indian—artifacts, a huge array of drums and cradle boards. (Go ahead and touch, she liked to say. Touch anything you want.) Most folks taking the tour did not realize that she had a smaller house downriver, closer to the city, up on the Palisades: a more manageable house in which she spent most of her free time, and that the actor's house, the one that for many years had been attached to her name by the general public, was mainly for show, or to make her feel a certain way. At the big house—nicknamed Wooden Nickel—she felt like the Grande Dame. At the other house—nicknamed Little Penny—she let her hair down and lay casually about and threw small, intimate dinner parties for her friends who came up from the city and admired her humility and the fact that someone so famous could live in such—and these were the words they used—limited circumstances, all the while knowing, of course, that she owned Wooden Nickel, too, along with Little Penny, and that she represented herself to the world—the general public—with Wooden Nickel and felt secure in doing so because she was not only the Grande Dame of Broadway but also a kind soul, altruistic and giving, and had shared the power of her wealth and fame more than most stars. Passing Wooden Nickel, those few who were aware that she owned Little Penny, and that she threw small parties there, were able to imagine both houses and to see the big house, with its widow's walk and stately facade and fantastic backyard—the pool, the guesthouse, the boathouse with the green light—those few were able to see Wooden Nickel in relation to the actress who also owned Little Penny. But even those souls, limited in number, still looked at the house and—if they were in a hurry—thought of her simply and cleanly. Whereas later, after the actor bought the house, if the same souls passed they made a single connection and thought only of him—the actor's house—because as far as anyone knew, it was his only residence. Not only was it his only house, but he lived there alone, too. So it took on the added weight of his isolation. He had moved there, most knew, after the divorce from his third wife, a famous beauty who had starred in a movie with him years earlier, a comedy about mismatched love: a young girl and a much older man who suffered from a form of autism that gave him (in the movie) an innate ability to communicate through his virtuosic piano playing.

(And watching that film they couldn't help but remember his old roles and the way, years before, his thick hands, tight in black gloves, had gripped the handlebars of his motorcycle while his hips shifted in his leather pants and his broad shoulders rolled gently beneath his T-shirts.) So passing the actor's house one might think, for no apparent reason, unable to pin down exactly why, about undershirts, and in doing so envision the old actor walking from room to room inside, head bowed, his big gut lurching, moving solemnly, stopping now and then to gaze out the window while he thought about some long-lost moment, a scene from one of his movies, maybe, in which he had embodied some character and given it life only to end up feeling, when the shot was finished, a sense of depletion and loss as he sank down into his chair bereft of whatever creative fuel and psychic juice it had taken to get himself into characters so far from himself—and not even real in the first place—that it seemed impossible, at times, to see across the chasm between the two states: as if he were now nothing but a husk of skin that had once contained those former characters. And it was easy to imagine, passing the house, that he felt empty and depleted all the time now, a remnant not only of his former self but also of his former characters. Eventually, almost everyone in the town who had known the Grande Dame and taken the annual open-house tour of Wooden Nickel forgot most of the details of the interior, with the exception, perhaps, of the cradle boards, and when passing the actor's house they were unable to completely imagine what it was like inside and could only conjure empty rooms defined by walls and the view of the river out the windows: the river, constantly changing, going from placid, glossy-smooth one morning—littered with trash and old tree limbs—and then ruffled with long flails of chop the next, always changing and never the same. So they found themselves limited, most of them, to imagining what the actor saw, if he actually looked from his back windows, when he sat alone and gazed out at the water, thinking about his past with a bitter sense of regret over the loss of his third wife, who was now dead, or the fact that he had squandered his career under the guise of being a genius, or perhaps because he really was a genius and did not know how to come to terms with the powers that came to him naturally and without study and made him feel uncomfortable: whereas (some passing the actor's house thought) if he had had to train hard and work at the acting, he might've felt a sense of proprietorship over his abilities (and, in turn, the house); whereas, some imagined, passing, he had been helplessly buoyant upon the raging sea of his talents so that, in turn, he could only garner a sense of control over his life by not acting, or by taking bit roles that were far beneath his talents, forcing his so-called genius into small, ill-fitting characters the same way he now squeezed into his ill-fitting clothes.

For a few years the actor's house did its best to maintain its former grandeur and to hold on to the Grande Dame for as long as it could, until eventually the windows began to warp out of their frames and the eaves sagged, chewed up by carpenter ants, and the paint began to scale along the clapboards. By the time the actor died, one windy fall afternoon, the house was fully his. On the day he died, those passing on the road glanced over and saw the house and perhaps thought: There's the actor's house, and then they thought about his films or looked ahead and simply went on their way, because he had lived there long enough in solitude, without showing his face, to nullify most speculation, and on that brisk fall day the structure had become, quite simply, the actor's house, and not much more.

SELF-PORTRAITS

by EIGHT WRITERS, FOUR FILMMAKERS, A MUSICIAN, A GRAPHIC DESIGNER, FOUR ACTORS, AND AN ARTIST

When I met the author Jonathan Ames in his office at Indiana University in late 2000, the only objects on his desk were a telephone and a stack of portrait doodles—some of them self-portraits. Ames had just begun his year in Bloomington as a visiting professor, and I'd dropped by to introduce myself and to ask if he'd contribute a story to my dorm-funded student literary magazine.

I never got around to asking for a story. Instead, after we'd talked awhile—Ames was very generous with his time—I asked about the doodles. Did he think of himself an artist? Not really. He compared the doodles to boogers. It can be fun to extract and admire a good one, he said (I paraphrase), before discarding it. When I asked if he'd let me publish some of them, he gamely handed me the whole stack, and we printed them all. It was fun.

A couple years ago, when I chanced upon a copy of Burt Britton's *Self-portraits*—a priceless book of doodles that Britton, a former bookseller, had solicited in the early 1970s from Norman Mailer, Jorge Luis Borges, Margaret Atwood, John Updike, and more than five hundred other writers—I fondly recalled Ames's booger doodles, and asked him to help me kick off a contemporary collection of self-portraits by talented creative people who may not be known for their drawing skills. Once again, Ames was game. Following are nineteen self-portraits from a book we're putting together at McSweeney's.

—*Brian McMullen*

Self-portrait
while st—ed...
looking in a mirror...
the beard is a bit
off but that's all right...
The expression of
fear and confusion
and stupidity
is
accurate.
Jonathan
Ames

M.L

FOUR
FOR
FORE
4

FUCK
embarassing start of shopping list before drawing...
manbrows
stache
weird vein
Sarah Silverman Self portrait

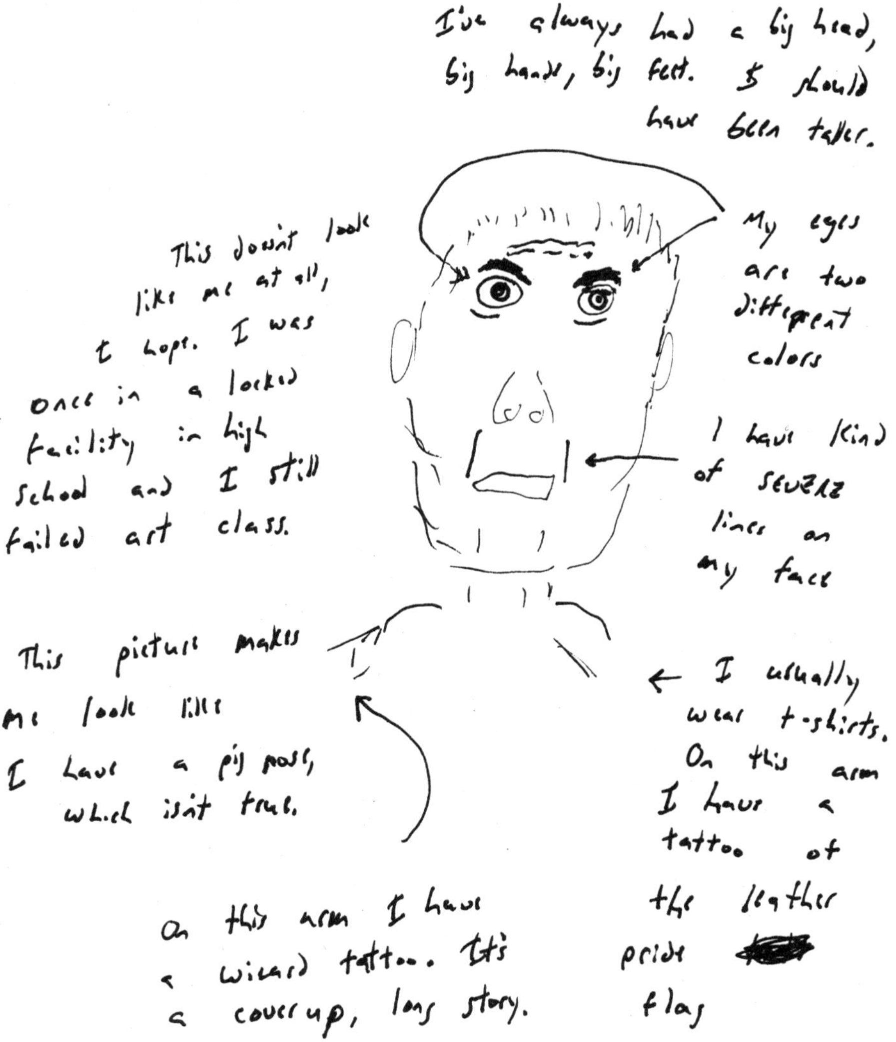

I've always had a big head, big hands, big feet. I should have been taller.
My eyes are two different colors
This doesn't look like me at all, I hope. I was once in a locked facility in high school and I still failed art class.
I have kind of severe lines on my face
This picture makes me look like I have a big nose, which isn't true.
I usually wear t-shirts. On this arm I have a tattoo of the leather pride flag
On this arm I have a wizard tattoo. It's a coverup, long story.

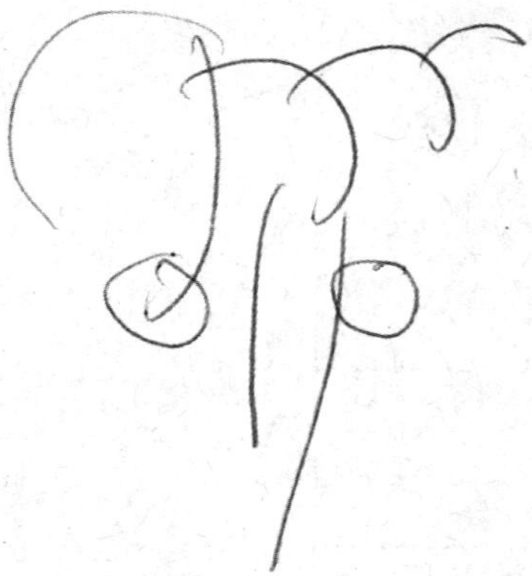

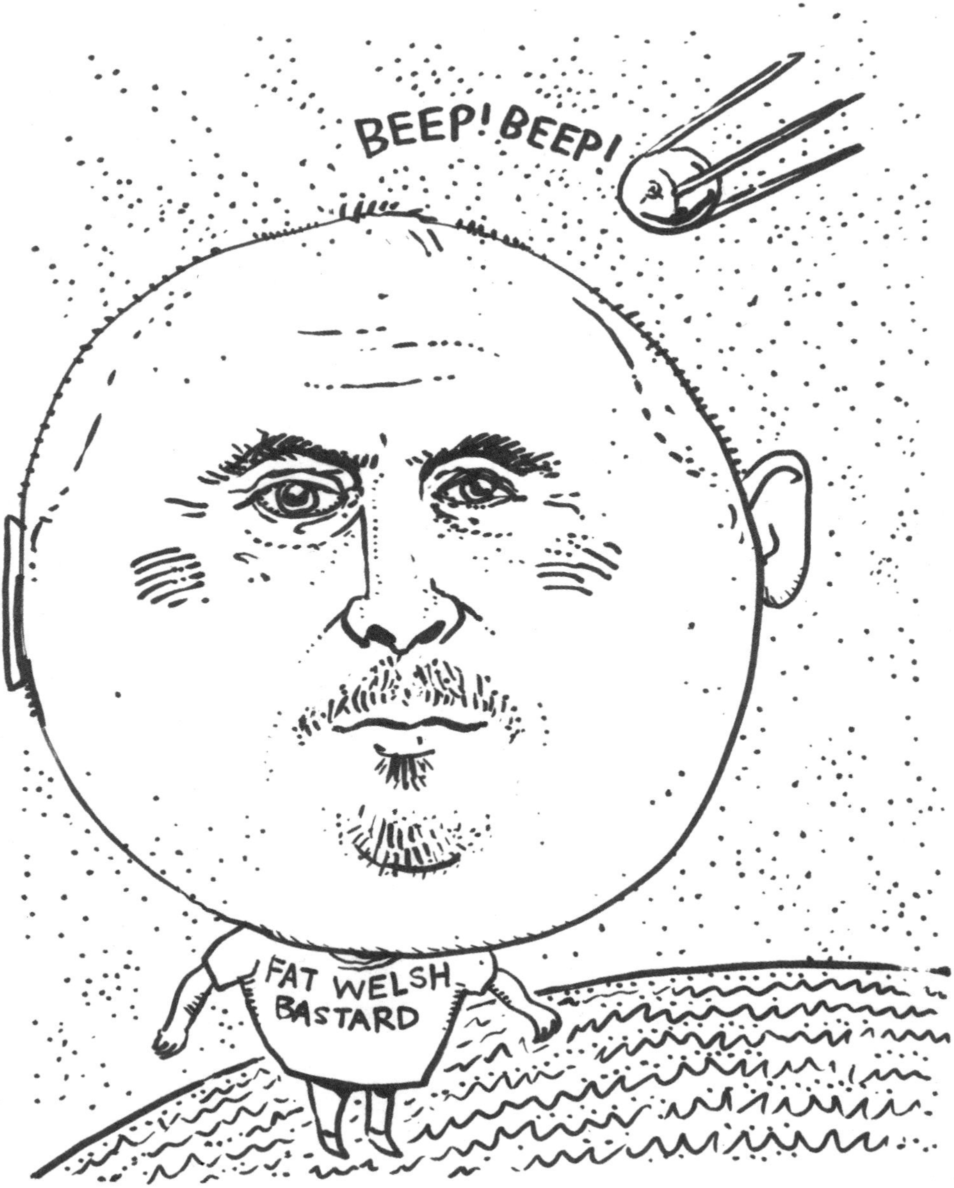
BEEP! BEEP!
FAT WELSH BASTARD

This is Jack Pendarvis

Ramin
Bahrani May 2009

Ben Marcus

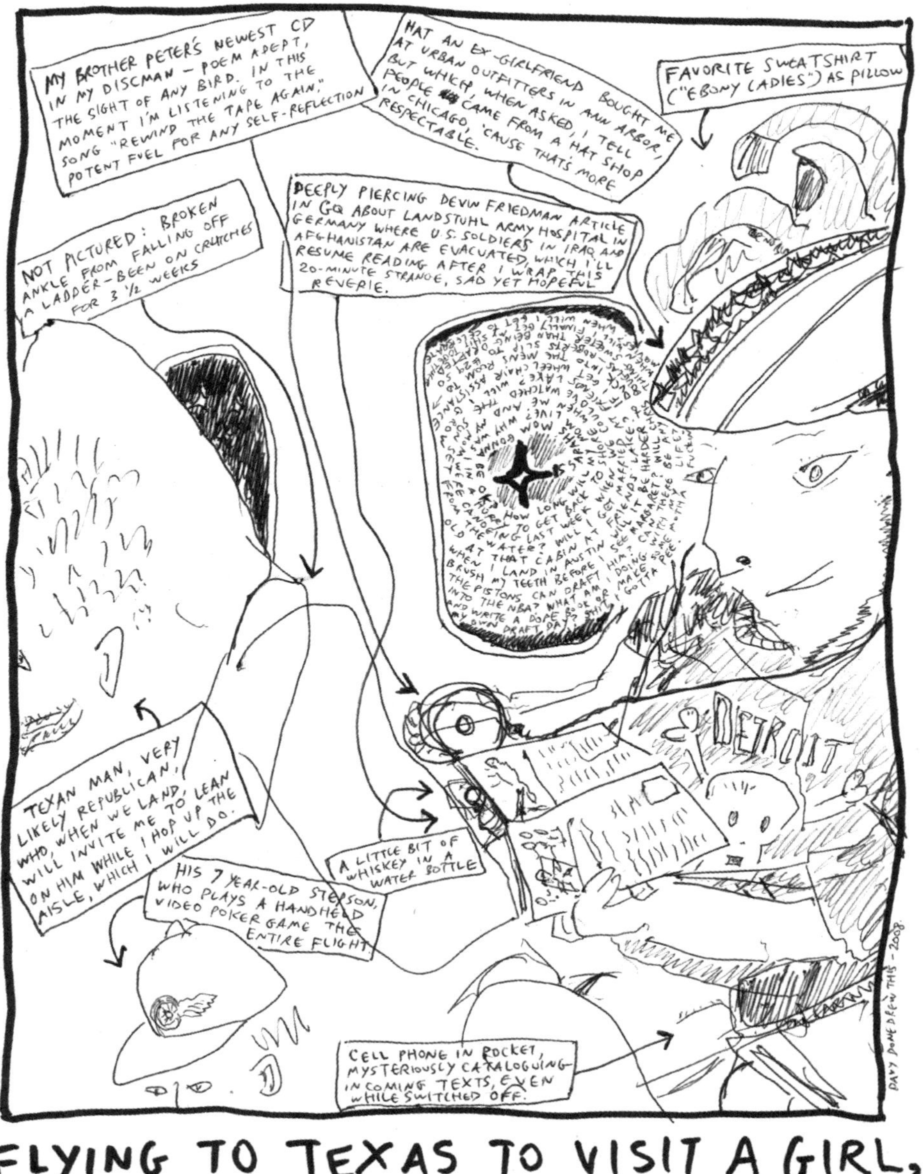

FLYING TO TEXAS TO VISIT A GIRL, LOOKING OUT THE WINDOW, LOST IN THOUGHT

THE WRECK OF THE *BEVERLY B.*

by T. Coraghessan Boyle

Picture her there in the pinched little galley where you could barely stand up without cracking your head, her right hand raw and stinging still from the scald of the coffee she'd dutifully—and foolishly—tried to make so they could have something to keep them going. She was wearing an oversized cableknit sweater she'd fished out of her husband's locker because the cabin was so cold, and every fiber of it seemed to chafe her skin as if she'd been flayed raw while she slept. She hadn't brushed her hair. Or her teeth. She was having trouble keeping her balance, wondering if it was always this rough out here, but she was afraid to ask Till about it, or Warren either. She didn't know the first thing about handling a boat or riding out a heavy sea or even reading a chart, as the two of them had been more than happy to remind her every chance they got. Her place was in the kitchen, they'd told her. Or rather, the galley. She was going to clean the fish and fry them, and when the sun came out—if it came out—she would spread a towel on top of the cabin and rub a mixture of baby oil and iodine on her legs, lie back, shut her eyes, and bask till they were a nice uniform brown.

It was only now, the boat pitching and rolling and her right hand vibrant with pain, that she realized that her feet were wet, her socks clammy and clinging and her new white tennis shoes gone a dark saturate gray. And why were her feet wet? Because there was water on the galley deck. Salt water. A thin bellying sheet of it riding toward her and jerking back as the boat pitched into another trough. She had to sit heavily then, the bench rising up to meet her while she clung to the tabletop with both hands, as helpless in that moment as if she were strapped into one of those lurching rides at the amusement park that Till seemed to love so much but that only made her feel as if her stomach had swallowed itself up like in that cartoon of the snake feeding its tail into its own jaws.

She tried to call out, but her throat squeezed shut. The water fled down the length of the deck and came back again, deeper, colder. *Do something!* she told herself. *Get up. Move!* Fighting down her nausea, she pulled herself around the table hand over hand so she could peer up the three steps to where Till sat at the helm, his bad arm rigid as a stick, while Warren, his brother Warren, the ex-Marine, bossy, know-it-all, shoved savagely at him, fighting him for the wheel. She wanted to warn them, wanted to betray the water in the galley so they could do something about it, so they could stop it, fix it, put things to right, but Warren was shouting, every vein standing out in his neck and the spray exploding over the stern behind him like the whipping tail of an underwater comet. "Goddamn you, goddamn you to hell! Keep the bow to the fucking waves!" The ship lurched sideways, shuddering down the length of it. "You want to see the whole goddamn shitbox go down?"

* * *

The month was March, the year 1946. Seaman First Class Tilden Matthew Boyd was six months home from the war in the Pacific that had left him with a withered right arm shorn of meat above the elbow, nothing there but a scar like a seared omelet wrapped around the bone. Beverly, young and hopeful and with hair as dark and abundant as any combed-out movie star's, broke a bottle over the bow of the *Beverly B.* while Till, restored to her from the vortex of the war in a miraculous dispensation more actual and solid than all the cathedrals in the world, sat at the helm and the gulls dipped overhead and the clouds swept in on a northwesterly breeze to chase the sun over the water. Beverly was happy because Till was happy, and they ate their sandwiches and drank the cheap champagne out of paper cups in the cabin because the wind was stiff and the chop wintry and white-capped. Warren was there too that first day, the day of the launching, a walking Dictaphone of unasked-for advice, ringing clichés, and long-winded criticism. But he drank the champagne and he showed up two weekends in a row to help Till tinker with the engines and install the teak cabinets and the fiddle rails Till had made in the garage of their rented house that needed paint and windowscreens for the mosquitoes and drainpipes to keep the winter rains from shearing off the roof and dousing anybody standing at the front door with a key in her hand and a load of groceries in both her aching arms. But Till had no desire to fix the house—it didn't belong to them anyway. The *Beverly B.*, though—that was a different story.

She was a sleek twenty-eight-foot all-wood cabin cruiser, solid-built, with butternut bulkheads and teak trim throughout, a real beauty, but she'd been dry-docked and neglected during the war, from which her owner, a Navy man, had never returned. Over the course of the fall and winter, Till had devoted himself to the task of refitting it, haunting the boatyard and the chandlery and fooling with the engines until he was so smudged with oil that Beverly told anybody who wanted to listen that half the time he looked like he was rigged out in blackface for some old-timey minstrel show. Her joke. Till in blackface. And she used it on Mrs. Viola down at the market and on Warren and on the girl he was seeing, Sandra, with the prim mouth and the sweaters she wore so tight you could see every line of her brassiere, straps and cups and all. Careful, that was what Till was. Careful and precise and unerring. He never mentioned it, never complained, but he'd given his right arm for his country and he was determined to keep the left one for himself. And for her. For her, above all.

He had to learn how to make it do the work of his right arm and wrist and hand, punching tickets for the Santa Monica Boulevard line while people looked on impatiently and tried to be polite out of a kind of grudging recognition, the dead hand clenching the ticket stub and the newly dominant one doing the punching, and he learned to use that hand to fold his paycheck over once and present it to her like a ticket itself, a ticket to a moveable feast to which she and she alone was invited. At night, late, after supper and the radio, he'd let the hand play over her nakedness as if it knew no impediment, and that was all right, that was as good as it was going to get, because he was left-handed now and always would be till the day he was gone. And when they launched the *Beverly B.* he was as gentle and cautious with his boat as he was with her in their marriage bed, the right arm swinging stiffly into play when the wheel revolved under pressure of the left, and the first few times they never took the boat out of sight of the harbor. Till said he wanted to get a feel for her, wanted to break her in, listen to what the twin Chrysler engines had to say when he pushed the throttle all the way forward and watched the tachometer climb to 2,800 rpm.

Then came that Friday evening late in March when she and Till and Warren motored out of the harbor on a course for the nearest of the northern Channel Islands, for Anacapa and the big one beyond it, Santa Cruz, because that was where the fish were, the lingcod as long as your arm, the abalone you only had to pluck off the rocks, abalone more plentiful than the rocks themselves, the lobsters so accommodating they'd crawl right up the anchor line and dunk themselves in the pot. A man at work had told Till all about it. Anybody could go out to Catalina—hell, everybody did go out there, day trippers and Saturday sailors and the rest—but if you wanted something akin to virgin territory, the northern islands, up off of Oxnard and Santa Barbara, that was the place to go. They'd brought along the two biggest ice chests she'd been able to find at Sears & Roebuck, both of them bristling with the dark slender necks of the beer bottles Warren assured her would have vanished by the time all those fish fillets and boiled lobsters were ready to nestle down there between their sheets of ice for a nice long sleep on the way home.

She'd made sandwiches at home—liverwurst on white with plenty of mustard and mayo, ham on rye, tuna fish salad—and when they settled down in the cabin to take big hungry bites out of them and wet their throats with the beer that was so cold it went down like mountain spring water, it was as if they'd fallen off the edge of the world. After dinner she'd sat out on the stern deck for a long while, the air sweet and unalloyed, everything still but for the steady thrum of the engines that was like the working of a sure steady heart, the heart at the center of the *Beverly B.*, unflagging and assured. There were dolphins, aggregations of them, silvered and pinked as they sluiced through the water and raced the hull to feel the electricity of it. They seemed to be grinning at her, welcoming her, as happy in their element as she was in hers. The last of the sun was tangled up in the mist ahead of them, due west and west the sun doth sink, the lines of a nursery rhyme scattered in her head. She lit a cigarette, the wind in her hair, and watched her husband through the newly washed windows as he held lightly to the wheel while his brother sat on the bench beside him, talking, always talking, but in dumb show now because the cabin door was shut and she couldn't hear a word.

She finished her cigarette and let the butt launch itself into the wind on a tail of red streamers. It was getting chilly, the sky darkening, closing around them like a lid set to an infinite iron pot. One more minute and she'd go in and listen to them talk, men's talk, about the pie in the sky, the fish in the sea, the carburetors and open-faced reels and lathes and varnishes and tools and brushes and calibrators that made them men, and she'd open another beer, too, a celebratory last beer to top off the celebratory three—or was it four?—she'd already had. It was then, just as she was about to rise, that the sea suddenly broke open like a dark spewing mouth and spat something at her, a hurtling shadowy missile that ran straight for her face till she snapped her head aside and it crashed with a reverberant wet thumping slap into the glass of the cabin door and both men wheeled round to see what it was.

She let out a scream. She couldn't help herself. This thing was alive and flapping there at her feet like some sort of sea bat, as long as her forearm, shivering now and springing up like a jack-in-the-box to fall back again and flap itself across the deck on the tripod of its wings and tail. Wings? It was—it was a fish, wasn't it? But here was Till, Warren bundled behind him, his face finding the middle passage between alarm and amusement, and he was stepping on the thing, slamming his foot down, hard, bending quickly to snatch the slick wet length of it up off the deck and hold it out to her like an offering in the grip of his good hand. "God, Bev, you gave me a scare—I thought you'd gone and pitched overboard with that scream."

Warren was laughing behind the sheen of merriment in his eyes. "This calls for a toast!" he shouted, raising the beer bottle that was perpetual with him. "Bev's caught the first fish!"

She was over her fright. But it wasn't fright—she wasn't one of those clinging weepy women like you saw in the movies. She'd just been startled, that was all. And who wouldn't have been, what with this thing, blue as gunmetal above and silver as a stack of coins below, coming at her like a torpedo with no warning at all? "Jesus lord," she said, "what *is* it?"

"Haven't you ever seen a flying fish before?" Till said. He made a clucking sound with his tongue. "Where've you been keeping yourself, woman?" he said, ribbing her. "This is no kitchen or sitting room or steam-heated parlor. You're out in the wide world now."

"A toast!" Warren crowed. "To Bev! A number-one fisherwoman!" And he was about to tip back the bottle when she took hold of his forearm, her hair whipping in the breeze. "Well then," she said, "in that case, I guess you're just going to have to get me another beer."

She woke dry-mouthed, a faint rising vapor lifting somewhere behind her eyes, as if her head had been pumped full of helium while she slept. In the berth across from her, snug under the bow as it skipped and hovered and rapped gently against the cushion of the waves, Till was asleep, his face turned to the wall which wasn't a wall but the planking of the hull of the ship that held them suspended over a black chasm of water. Below her, down deep, there were things immense and minute, whales, copepods, sharks and sardines, crabs infinite—the bottom alive with them in their horny chitinous legions, tearing the flesh from drowned things and feeding the scraps into the shearing miniature shredders of their mouths. All this came to her in the instant of waking, without confusion or dislocation—she wasn't in the double bed they were still making payments on or stretched out on the narrow mattress in the spare room at her parents' house where she'd waited through a thousand hollow echoing nights for Till to come home and reclaim her. She was at sea. She knew the rocking of the boat as intimately now as if she'd never known anything else, felt the muted drone of the engines deep inside her, in the thump of her heart and the pulse of her blood. At sea. She was at sea.

She sat up. A shaft of moonlight cut through the cabin behind her, slicing the table in two. Beyond that, a dark well of shadow, and beyond the shadow the steps to the bridge and the green glow of the controls where Warren, with his bunched muscles and engraved mouth, sat piloting them through the night. She needed—urgently—to use the lavatory. The head, that is. And water—she needed a glass of water from the tap in the head that was attached to the forty-gallon tank in the hold that Till had made such a fuss about because you couldn't waste water, not at sea, where you never knew when you were going to get more. It had got to the point where she was almost afraid to turn on the tap for fear of losing a single precious drop. What was that poem from high school? "Water, water, every where / Nor any drop to drink."

Her bare feet swung out of the berth. The deck was solid, cool, faintly damp. She was wearing a flannel nightgown that covered her all the way to her toes, though she wished she'd been able to wear something a little sheerer for Till's sake—but that would have to wait until they were back home in the privacy of their own bedroom. She was modest and decent, not like the other girls who'd gone out and cheated on their overseas men the first chance they got, and she just didn't feel comfortable showing herself off in such close quarters with Warren there, even if he was Till's brother. She'd seen the way Warren looked at her sometimes, and it was no different from what she'd had to endure since she'd begun to develop in the eighth grade, leers and wolf whistles and all the rest.

She slipped into the head, used the toilet, drained her glass of water and then drained another. She cranked the hand pump to flush, rinsed her hands—precious water, precious—eased the door open, and shut it behind her.

When she woke again it was daylight and Till's berth was empty. She tried to focus on the deck but the deck wouldn't stay put. A great angry fist seemed to be slamming at the hull with a booming repetitive shock that concussed the thin mattress and the plank beneath it and worked its way through her until she could feel it in the hollow of her chest, in her head, in her teeth. On top of it, every last thing, every screw and bolt and scrap of metal up and down the length of the boat, rattled and whined with a roused insistent drone as if a hive of yellow jackets was trapped in the hull. And what was that smell? Mold, hidden rot, the sour-milk reek of her own unwashed body. Before she could think, she was leaning over and spewing up everything inside her into the bucket she'd kept at her bedside for emergencies—the last of it, sharp and acerbic as a dose of vinegar, coming on a long glutinous string of saliva. She shook her head to clear it, wiped her mouth on the back of her hand. Then she got up, fumbling for her blue jeans and a sweater, Till's sweater, rough as burlap but the warmest thing she could find, and how had it gotten so cold?

It took her a while, just sitting there and picturing dry land, a beach on the island, a rock offshore, anything that wasn't moving, before she was able to get up and work her way into the galley. She filled the percolator with water, poured coffee into the strainer directly from the can without bothering to measure it—she could barely stand, let alone worry about the niceties, and they'd want it strong in any case—and then she set the pot on the burner, but it kept tilting and sliding till she hit on the idea of wedging it there with the big cast-iron pot she intended to make chowder in when they got where they were going. If they ever got there. And what had happened? Had the weather gone crazy all of a sudden? Was it a typhoon? A hurricane?

She looked a fright, she knew it, and she'd have to do something about her hair, but she worked her way up the juddering steps to the bridge and flung herself down on the couch there—or the bench she'd converted to a couch by sewing ties to a set of old plaid cushions she'd found in her parents' garage. The cabin was close, breath-steamed, smelling of men's sweat and the muck at the bottom of the sea. Till was right there, just across from her, sitting in his chair at the controls, so near she could have reached out and touched him. The wheel jumped and jumped again, and he fought it with his left hand while forcing the throttle forward and back in the clumsy stiff immalleable grip of the other one. Warren leaned over him, grim-faced. Neither seemed to have noticed her.

It was only then that she became aware of the height of the waves coming at them, rearing black volcanoes of water that took everything out from under the boat and put it right back again, all the while blasting the windows as if there were a hundred fire trucks out there with their hoses all turned on at once. And here was the rhythm, up, down, up, and a rinse of the windows with every repetition. "Where are we?" she heard herself ask.

Till never looked up. He was frozen there, nothing moving but his arms and shoulders. "Don't know," Warren said, glancing over his shoulder. "Halfway between Anacapa and Santa Cruz, but with the way this shit's blowing, who could say?"

She looked out ahead of them to where the bow dipped to its pounding, but she couldn't see anything but waves, one springing up off the back of the other, infinite and impatient, coming and coming and coming. Her stomach fell. She thought she might vomit again, but there was nothing left to bring up. "What happened to the weather?" she asked, raising her voice to be heard over the wind, but it wasn't a question really, more an observation in search of some kind of assurance. She wanted them to tell her that this was nothing they couldn't handle, just a little blow that would peter out before long, after which the sun would come back to illuminate the world and all would be as calm and peaceful as it had been last night, when the waves lapped the hull and the sandwiches and beer went down and stayed down in the pure pleasure of the moment. No one answered. She wasn't scared, not yet, because all this was so new to her and because she trusted Till—Till knew what he was doing. He always did. "I put on coffee," she said, though the thought of it, of the smell and taste of it and the way it clung viscously to the inside of the cup in a discolored slick, made her feel weak all over again. "You boys"—she had to force the words out—"think you might want a cup?"

Then she was back down in the galley, banging her elbows and knees, flung from one position to another, and when she reached for the coffeepot it jumped off the stove of its own volition and scalded her right hand. Before she could register the shock of it, the pot was on the deck, the top spun off and the steaming grounds and six good cups of black coffee spewed across the galley. Her first thought was for the deck—the coffee would stain, eat through the varnish like acid—and before she looked to her burn she was down on her hands and knees, caroming from one corner of the cabin to the other like the silver ball in a pinball machine, dabbing at the mess as she went by with a rag that became so instantaneously and unforgivingly hot she burned her hand a second time. When finally she'd got the deck cleaned up as best she could, she fell back into the bench at the table, angry now, angry at the boat and the sea and the men who'd dragged her out here into this shitty little rattling sea-stinking jail cell, and she swore she'd never go out again, never, no matter what promises they made. "There'll be no coffee, and I'm sorry, I am," she said aloud. "You hear that?" she called out, directing her voice toward the steps at the back of the cabin. "No coffee today, no breakfast, no nothing. I'm through!"

The pain of the burn sparked then, assailing her suddenly with an insidious throbbing and prickling, the blisters already forming and bursting, and she thought of getting up and rubbing butter into the reddened flesh on the back of her hand and between her scalded fingers, but she couldn't move for the boat shaking.

That was when the water started coming in through the forward hatch. That was when her feet got wet and she began to feel afraid. That was when she thought for the first time of the life jackets tucked in under the seats in the stern that was awash with the piled-up waves—and that was when she pulled herself along the edge of the table to look up into the bridge and see her husband and brother-in-law fighting over the controls even as she heard the engines sputter and catch and finally give out. She caught her breath. Something essential had gone absent in a way that was wrong, deeply wrong, in violation of everything she'd known and believed in since the moment they'd left shore. The ghost had gone out of the machine.

In a moment she was on the bridge, trying to make Till and Warren understand about the water in the cabin, water that didn't belong there, water that was coming in through a breach in the forward hatch that was underwater itself before it shook free of the weight of the waves and then sank back down again. But Till wasn't listening. Till, her rock, the man who'd survived the mangling of his arm and the fiery blast of shrapnel that was lodged still in his legs and secreted beneath the constellation of scars on the broad firmament of his back, sat slumped over the controls, distracted and drawn and punching desperately at the starter as Warren, wrapped in a yellow slicker and cursing with every breath, fought his way out the door to the stern while the wind sang through the cabin and all the visible world lost its substantiality.

The boat lolled, staggered, a wave rising up out of nowhere to hit them broadside and drive down the hull till she was sure they were going to capsize. She might have screamed. Might have cried out uselessly, her breath coming hard and fast. It was all she could do to hold on, her jaws clamped, the spray taking flight up and over the cabin as Warren pried open the hatch to the engine compartment, some sort of tool clutched in one hand—Warren, Warren out there on the deck to save the day, but what could he hope to do? How could anybody fix anything in this chaos?

He was a blotch of yellow in a world stripped of color, there one moment and gone the next, a big breaching wave flinging him back against the cabin door and pouring half an ocean into the rictus of the engine well. Till snatched a look at her then, his face drained and hopeless. Warren, the figure of Warren, flailing limbs and gasping mouth, slammed at the window and rose impossibly out of the foam, the slicker twisted back from his shoulders—inadequate, ridiculous, a child's jacket, a doll's—and then he was down again and awash. In the next instant Till sprang to his feet, twisting up and away from the controls, the wheel swinging wildly, lights blinking across the console, the scuppers inundated, the bilge pump choking on its own infirmity. He took hold of her wrist, jerking her up out of her seat, and suddenly they were through the door and into the fury of the weather, the wind tearing the breath out of her lungs, the next wave rearing up to knock her to her knees with a fierce icy slap, and she wasn't sick anymore and she wasn't tired or worn or dulled. Everything in her, everything she was, howled at its highest pitch. They were going to drown, all three of them, she could see that now. Drown and die and wash up for the crabs.

"What do you think you're doing?" Warren, unsteady, hair painted to his face, made to seize Till's arms as if he meant to dance with him, even as Till shrugged him off and bent to release the skiff.

"It's our only chance!" Till roared into the wind, his legs tangled and rotating out of sync like a drunken man's. He flailed at the shell of the skiff, jerked the lines in a fury.

"You're nuts!" Warren shouted. "Out of your fucking mind!" He was reeling too, fighting for balance, and so was she, helpless, the waves driving at her. The boat heaved, dead beneath their feet. "We won't last five minutes in this sea!"

But here was the skiff, released and free and riding high, and they were in it, and the *Beverly B.* was swamped. Stalled. Going down.

Heavily, like a waterlogged post in a swollen river, the boat shifted away from them. They'd painted her hull white to contrast with the natural wood of the cabin—a cold pure unblemished white, the white of sheets and carnations—and that whiteness shone now like the ghost image on a negative of a photograph that would never be developed. Unimpeded, the waves crashed at the windows of the cabin and then the glass was gone and the *Beverly B.* shifted wearily and dropped down and came back up again. The decks were below water now, only the cabin's top showing pale against the dimness of the early morning and the spray that rode the wind like a shroud.

Beverly was there to witness it, huddled wet and shivering in the bow of the skiff, Till beside her, but she wasn't clinging to him, not clinging at all because she was too rigid with the need to get out of this, to get away, to get to land. No regrets. Let the sea have the boat and all the time and money they'd lavished on her, so long as it spared them, so long as the island was out there in the gloom and it came to them in a rush of foam and black bleeding rock. They rode up over two waves, three, and they were on a wild ride now, wilder than anything the amusement park would ever dare offer, and all at once they were in a deep pit lined with walls of aquamarine glass, everything held suspended for a single shimmering moment before the walls collapsed on them. She felt the plunge, the force of it, and all of a sudden she was swimming free, the chill riveting her, and it was instinct that drove her away from the skiff and back to the *Beverly B.* for something to hold fast to—and there, there it was, rising up and plunging down, and she with it.

She didn't see Warren, didn't see where he was, but then she'd got turned around and he could be anywhere. And Till—she remembered him coming toward her, his good arm cutting the black sheet of the water, until he wasn't coming anymore. Where was he? The waves threw up ramparts and she couldn't see. He was calling her, she was sure of it, in the thinnest distant echo of a cracked and winnowed voice, Till's voice, sucked away on the wind until it was gone. "Where are you?" she called. "Till? Till?"

The waves took her breath away. Her bones ached. Her teeth wouldn't stop chattering. A period of time elapsed—she couldn't have said how long—and nothing changed. She clung to the heaving corpse of the *Beverly B.* because the *Beverly B.* was the only thing there was. At some point, because they were binding her feet, she ducked her head beneath the surface to tear off her tennis sneakers and release them into the void. Then she loosed her blue jeans, the cuffs as heavy as lead weights.

When finally the *Beverly B.* cocked herself up on a wave as big as a continent and then sank down out of sight, she fought away from the vortex it left in its wake and found herself treading water. The waves lifted and released her, lifted and released her. She was alone. Deserted. The ship gone, Till gone, Warren. She could feel something flapping inside her like a set of wings, her own panic, the panic that whipped her into a sudden slashing breaststroke and as quickly subsided, and then she was treading water again and she went on treading water for some portion of eternity till there was nothing left in her arms. Till's sweater dragged at her. It was too much, too heavy, and it gave her nothing, not warmth, not comfort, not Till or the feel or smell of him. She shrugged out of it, snatched a breath, and let it drift down and away from her like the exoskeleton of a creature new-made, born of water and salt and the penetrant chill.

She tried floating on her back but the wind drove the sea up her nose and into her mouth. She came up coughing and spewing. She fought the rising fear with her spent arms and the feeble wash of her spent legs. After a time she lost all feeling in her limbs and she went down with a lungful of air and the air brought her back up, once, twice, again. She thrashed for a handhold, for anything, for substance, but there was no solid thing in all that transient medium where the dolphins grinned and the flying fish flew.

And Till? Where was Till? He could have been right there, ten feet away, and she wouldn't have known it. She closed her eyes, snatched a breath, let herself drift down and let herself come back again. Once more. Could she do it once more? She'd never known despair, but it was in her now, colder than the water, creeping numbly up from her feet and into her ankles and legs and torso, overwhelming her, claiming her degree by degree. *Water, water every where.* Just as she was about to surrender, to open herself up, open wide and let the harsh insistent unforgiving current flow through her and tug her down to where the waves couldn't touch her ever again, the ocean gave her something back: it was a chest, an ice chest, floating low in the water under the weight of its burden. A silver thing, silver as the belly of her fish. Sears & Roebuck. Guaranteed for life. She claimed it as her own, and though she couldn't get atop it, it was there and it sustained her as the wind bit and the sun rose up out of the gloom to parch her lips and scorch the taut white mask of her upturned face.

* * *

She had never been so thirsty in all her life. Had never known what it was, what it truly meant, because she'd lived in a house with a tap in a place where the grass was wet with dew in the morning and you could get a Coca-Cola at any lunch counter or in the machine at the service station around the corner. If she was thirsty, she drank. That was all.

Now she knew. Now she knew what it was like to go without, to feel the talons clawing at your throat, the tongue furred and bloating in the tomb of your mouth, barely able to swallow, to breathe. There was ice in the chest—and beer, chilled beer, the bottles clinking and chirping with the rhythm of the waves—but she didn't dare crack the lid, even for an instant. It was the air inside that kept her afloat, and if she lifted the lid the air would rush out and where would she be then? The bottles clinked. This was a special brand of torture, reserved just for her, worse than anything devised by the most sadistic Jap commandant, and she kept wondering what she'd done to deserve it—the ice right there, the beer, the sweet cold sparkling pale golden liquid in the bottle that would shine with condensation just inches away, and she dying of thirst.

She swallowed involuntarily at the thought of it, the lining of her throat as raw as when she'd had tonsillitis as a girl and twisted in agony with the blinds closed and the starched rigid sheets biting into her till her mother came like an angel of mercy with ginger ale in a tall cold glass, with sherbet, Jell-O, ice cubes made of Welch's grape juice to suck and roll over her tongue and clench between her teeth till all the moisture was gone. Her mother's hand reached out to her, she saw it, saw it right there framed against the waves, and her mother's face and the dripping glass poised in her hand. It was too much to bear. She gave in and wet her lips with seawater, though she knew she shouldn't, knew it was wrong and would only make things worse, and yet she couldn't help herself, her tongue probing and lapping as if it weren't attached to her at all. The relief was instantaneous, flooding her like a drug—water, there was water inside her. But then, almost immediately, her throat swelled shut and her cracked lips began to bleed.

To bleed. That was the secondary problem: blood. Both her elbows were scraped and raw and there was a deep irregular gash on the back of her left hand, the one the scalding coffee hadn't touched. How it had got there she couldn't say, and she was so numb from the cold she couldn't feel the sting of it, though clearly it would need stitches to close the wound and there'd be a scar, and for some time now she'd been idly examining the torn flesh there, thinking she'd have to see a doctor when they got back and already making up a little speech for him, how she'd want a really top-notch man because she just couldn't stomach having her skin spoiled, not at her age. But she was bleeding in the here and now, each wave washing the gash anew and extracting from it a pale tincture of pinkish liquid that dissolved instantly and was gone. That liquid was blood. And blood attracted sharks.

Again the flap of panic. Her legs trailed behind her like lures, like a provocation, like bait, and she couldn't see them, could barely feel them. If the sharks came—*when* they came—she'd have no defense. She was trapped in a childhood nightmare, a vestigial dream of the time before there was land, when all the creatures there were floated free amidst the flotilla of shining jaws that would swallow them. She tried to hold her hand up out of the water. Tried not to think about what was beneath her, behind her, rising even now from the lazy depths like a balloon trailing across the sky at dusk. But she had to think. Had to terrify herself just to stay alive.

She'd seen a shark only once in her life. It was on the Santa Monica pier, just after Till had come home from overseas. They'd walked on the beach for hours and then promenaded all the way to the end of the pier, her arm in his, the stripped pale boards rocking gently beneath their feet and the sea air deliciously cool against their skin. She was so alive in that moment, so attuned to Till and his transformation from the recollected to the actual, to the flesh, to the arm round her waist and the voice murmuring in her ear, that the smallest things thrilled her with their novelty, as if no one had ever conceived of them before. A paper cone of cotton candy, so intensely pink it was otherworldly, seemed as strange to her as if it had been delivered there from outer space. Ditto the tattooed man exhibiting himself in his bathing trunks in the hope of spare change, and the eighty-year-old beauty queen in the two-piece—even the taste of the burger with chopped raw onions and plenty of catsup they ate standing under the sunstruck awning of the stand at the foot of the pier was like no other burger she'd ever had. Her feet weren't even on the ground. They were there in the flesh, both of them, she and Till, strolling along like any normal couple who could go home to bed anytime the urge took them, day or night, or go get a highball and listen to the jukebox in the corner of some dark roadhouse or drive slow and sweet along Ocean Boulevard with the windows down and the breeze fanning their hair. It was her dream made concrete. But then, right there in the middle of that dream, was the shark.

There was a crowd gathered at the far end of the pier and they'd gone toward it casually, out of idle curiosity, people looping this way and that, little kids squirming through to the front for a closer view, and there it was, more novelty, the first shark she'd ever seen outside of a picture book. It was suspended by its tail on a thick braid of cable that held it, dripping, just above the bleached boards of the dock. The fisherman—a Negro, and that was a novelty too, a Negro fisherman on the Santa Monica pier—stood just off to the left of it while his companion, another Negro, took his photograph with a Brownie camera. "Hold steady now," the second man said. "Less have a smile. C'mon, give us a grin."

A woman beside her made a noise in her throat, an admixture of disgust and fascination. "What is it?" the woman said. "A swordfish?"

The first man, the fisherman, smiled wide and the camera clicked. "You see a sword?" he asked rhetorically. "I don't see no sword. What this is, what you looking at right now? This a great white shark, seven feet six inches long. As bad as it gets. And this one's not much more than a baby. Hell, they five feet long when they come out their mother."

The crowd pressed in. Till's eyes were gleaming, and this was a thing he could appreciate, a man's thing, *as bad as it gets*. The image had stayed with her a long while.

People died of shark bite. They died of thirst. Of hypothermia. She was dressed in nothing but bra and panties, naked to the water and the water sucking the heat from her minute by minute, and she clung there and shivered and felt the volition go out of her. Let the sharks come, she was thinking, dreaming, the cold lulling her now till she woke sputtering, choked awake, a cold fist in her throat. She was coughing—hacking, heaving, retching—and the violence of it brought her back again. Sun, sea, wind, waves. Sun. Sea. Wind. Waves. The ice chest bobbed and she bobbed with it. And then, all at once, there was something else there with her, something new, a living thing that broke the surface in a fierce boiling suddenness that annihilated her, the shark, the shark come finally to draw the shroud. She shut her eyes, averted her face. She didn't draw up her legs because there was no point in it now, the drop was coming, the first rending shock of the jaws, sadness spreading though her like a stain in water, sadness for Till, for her parents, for what might have been... but the next moment slipped by and the moment after that and still she was there and still she was whole, bobbing along with the ice chest, bobbing.

The next splash was closer. She forced open her eyes, tried to focus through the drooping curtains of her swollen lids. Her pupils burned. The blood pounded in her ears. It took her a moment to understand that this wasn't a shark, wasn't a fish at all—fish didn't have dog faces and whiskers and eyes as round and darkly glowing as a human's. She stared into those eyes, amazed, until they sank away in the wash and she looked beyond the swirl of foam to the sun-scoured wall of rock rising out of the mist above her.

Anacapa is the smallest of the four islands that form the archipelago of the northern Channel Islands and the closest to the mainland, a mere eleven miles from its eastern tip to the harbor at Oxnard. In actuality, Anacapa comprises three separate islets, connected only during extreme low tides, and is of volcanic origin, composed primarily of basalt dating from the Miocene period. All three islets are largely inaccessible from the sea, featuring tall looming circumvallate cliffs and strips of cliffside beach that darkly glisten with the detritus ground out of the rock by the action of the waves. Average rainfall is less than twelve inches annually. There is no permanent source of water.

Beverly knew none of this. She didn't know that the landfall looming over her was Anacapa or that she'd drifted some six miles by this point. She knew only that rock was solid and water was not and she made for it with all the strength left in her. Twice she went under and came up gasping and it was all she could do to keep hold of the ice chest in the roiling surf that had begun to crash round her. All at once she was in the breakers and the chest was torn from her, gone suddenly, and she had no choice but to squeeze her eyes shut and extend her arms and ride the wave till the force of it flung her like so much wrack at the base of the cliff. Stones rolled and collided beneath her knees and the frantic grabbing of her hands, she was tossed sideways and felt the breath pounded out of her, but her fingers snatched at something else there, sand, the floor of a beach gouged out of the rock. It was nothing more than a semicircular pit, churning like a washing machine, but it was palpable and it held her and when the wave sucked back she was standing on solid ground. She might have felt a surge of relief, but she didn't have a chance. She was shivering. Dripping. Staggering. And the next wave was already coming at her.

The foam shot in, sudsing at her knees, driving her back awkwardly against the punishing black wall of the overhang. She found herself stumbling to her left even as the next breaker thundered in, and then she was crawling on hands and knees up and away from it, the rock pitted and sharp and yet slick all the same, up and out of the water and onto a narrow perch that was no wider than her berth on the *Beverly B.* She hugged her knees to her chest, clamped her hands round her shoulders, shook with cold. Her hair hung limp in her face. The waves crashed and dissolved into mist and everything smelled of funk and rot and the protoplasmic surfeit of all those galaxies of wheeling, biting, wanting things that hadn't survived the day. She didn't think about Till or the boat or Warren. Her mind was drawn down to nothing. She just stared numbly at the wash as it stripped the beach and gave it back again, torn strands of kelp struggling to and fro, a float of driftwood, the suck and roar, and then she was asleep.

When she woke it was to the sun and the beach that had grown marginally bigger, a scallop of blackly glistening sand emerging from the receding tide, the teeth of the rocks exposed now and the wet gums clamped beneath them. She'd been in the shadows all this time, huddled on her perch, tucked away from the tidal wash and the sun too, but now the sun had moved out into the channel and the heat of it touched her and roused her. And then, abruptly, she was thirsty. Still thirsty. Thirstier than she'd been out there on the sea when she was thirstier than she'd ever been in her life.

In that moment her eye jumped to the gleam of metal at the near end of the cove. The ice chest. There it was, upright in the sand, its lid still fastened. She sprang down from the rock, slimed and filthy, her limbs battered and her tongue made of felt, and ran to it, tore back the lid and saw that the ice was gone and the bottles smashed—all but one, the precious last remaining dark brown sweating bottle with the label soaked off and sand worked up under the cap. Lifting the beer to the sun, she could see that it was intact, its bubbles infused with light and rising in a slow hypnotic dance. *Beer. Cold beer.* But she had no opener, no churchkey, no knife or screwdriver or tool of any kind.

Rock. Rock would do it. Of course it would. And then she was smoothing her hand over the wall of the overhang, feeling for a rough spot, a ledge, any kind of projection, and here, here it was, the cap poised just so and the weight of her burned hand coming down on it, once, twice... and nothing. She worked at it, frantic now, angry, furious, but the best she could do was flatten the ridges till the cap was even more secure than when she'd begun, and it was too much, she couldn't take a single second more of this—and then it was done, the neck shattered and gaping and she draining the whole thing in three airless gulps and if there was glass in it and if the glass cut her open from esophagus to gut she didn't give a damn because she was drinking and that was the only thing that mattered.

But the beer was gone and the thirst was there still, rattling inside her like a field of cane in a desert wind, and was it any surprise she was lightheaded? She'd always been a capable drinker, proud of her ability to match Till beer for beer, but this one hit her hard and before she knew it she was down in the sand, sitting there cross-legged like a statue of the Buddha, as if that was what she'd meant to do all along. The sun seemed to have shifted somehow in the interval, dropping down close to the flattening gray surface of the sea where the fog could take hold of it and snuff it out like the burned-up butt of the cigarette she suddenly wanted as much as she wanted water. She stood shakily and went to the ice chest. It was right where she'd left it not ten minutes ago (or had it been longer? Had she dozed off?), but now the incoming tide was running up the beach to take it from her all over again. Seizing it by one corner, she dragged it awkwardly across the sand to the declivity beneath the overhang, then worked it up to her perch six feet above the beach. Inside, amidst the litter of broken bottles and stripes of sand and weed, there was a liquid that might have been a mix of beer and meltwater, that might have been potable, that might have quenched her thirst, but when she thrust a finger into it and licked that finger all she could taste was salt.

Dusk fell, aided and abetted by the fog, which closed off the beach even as the tide ran in, and though the water was up past her knees she probed the scalloped ledges at both ends of the cove, looking for a way out. She braced herself, one foot up, then the other, straining for a handhold. Working patiently, her face pressed to the rock, she got as high as fifteen or twenty feet above the beach, but after she fell for the third time, coming down hard amid the litter and the cold shock of the water, she gave up. It was no use. She was trapped. She wasn't afraid, not anymore—that was behind her. All she felt was frustration. Anger. Why had she been spared only to wash up here to die of thirst, hunger, cold? Where was God's hand in that? Where was His purpose? Finally, when it was fully dark and the fog settled in so impenetrably as to close off even the stars, let alone the running lights of any boat that might have been plying the channel looking for them, for survivors—and here she saw Till and Warren, wrapped in blankets in a gently rocking cabin, the glow of the varnished wood, lanterns a-sway, mugs of hot coffee pressed to their lips—she held fast to the ice chest and willed herself asleep.

In the morning, at first light, there was the sound of the gulls that was like the opening and closing of a door on recalcitrant hinges, but there was no door here, no bed or room or clothes or warmth, and she couldn't see the gulls for the fog. She shivered into the light, slapping at her thighs and shoulders and huddling in the cradle of her arms, and it took her a long moment to realize that there was a persistent cold drip tapping at her shoulder and that she'd been shifting unconsciously to avoid it. She lifted her face and saw that the cliff was wet, the fog whispering across the rock above her, condensing there, dripping, dripping.

She held her tongue out to it, licked the rock as if it were a snow cone presented to her by the lady behind the concession stand at the county fair. And when one of the little green shore crabs came within reach, a flattened thing, no more than two inches across, she crushed it beneath her foot and then fed the salty cold wet fragments into her mouth.

It took her a long while after that to get her courage up, because she knew now what she had to do, though her whole being revolted against it. She kept praying that someone would come for her, that the prow of a ship would ease out of the fog or a rope come hurtling down from above, anything to spare her getting back into that killing water. The funny thing was that she'd always liked swimming—she'd joined the swim team in school and trained so relentlessly her hair never seemed to be really dry her whole senior year—but now, as she climbed down from the rock, clutched the ice chest to herself and fought through the surf, she hated it more than anything in the world. Instantly, she was cold through to the bone and thrashing for warmth, and then she was fighting past the breakers and out into the sea.

Here was the nightmare all over again, but this time there was a difference because she was saved, she'd saved herself, and she kept close to shore, trembling, yes, exhausted, thirsty, but no longer panicked. There wouldn't be sharks, not this close in; if there were, the sea wouldn't be full of seals, armies of them barking from the rocks and sending up a sulfurous odor of urine and feces and seal stink. The sea was calmer now too, much calmer—almost gentle—and from time to time she tried floating on her back, head propped on the chest and elbows jackknifed behind her, but invariably she had to roll over and pull herself up as far as she could in an effort to escape the cold.

She let the current carry her, periodically forcing herself to unfurl her legs and paddle to keep on course, telling herself that at any moment she'd come upon a boat at anchor or a beach that spread back to a canyon where she could get up and away from the sea. How far she'd drifted or how long she'd been in the water she had no way of knowing, the cold sapping her, lulling her, killing her will, every seal-strewn rock and every black-faced cliff so exactly like the last one she began to think she'd circled the island twice already.

It must have been late in the morning, the sun lost somewhere in the fog overhead, when finally she found what she was looking for. Or rather, she didn't know what she was looking for until it materialized out of the haze in a cove that was no different from all the rest. A rust-peached ladder, so oxidized it was the color of the starfish clinging to the rocks beneath it, seemed to glide across the surface toward her. When she took hold of it she let the ice chest float free, pulling herself from the water, rung by rung, as from a gently yielding sheath.

The universe stopped rocking. The sea fell away. And she found herself on a path leading steeply upward to where the fog began to tatter and bleed off till it wasn't there at all. Above her, opening to the sun and the chaparral flecked with yellow blooms that climbed beard-like up the slope, was a shack, two shacks, three, four, all lined up across the bluff as if they'd grown out of the rock itself. The near one—flat-roofed, the boards weathered gray—caught the flame of the sun in its windows till it glowed like a cathedral. And right beside it, where the drainpipe fell away from the roof, was a wooden barrel, a hogshead, set there to catch the rain.

She was in that moment reduced to an animal, nothing more. Her focus was an animal's focus, her mind stripped of everything but that barrel and its contents, and she never felt the fragmented stone of the path digging into her feet or the weight of the sun crushing her shoulders till she reached it and plunged her face into its depths and drank till she could feel the cool silk thread coming back up again. It was only then that she looked around her. Everything was still, hot, though she shivered in the heat, and her first thought was to call out, absurdly, "Hello? Is anybody there?" Or why not "Yoo-hoo?" Yoo-hoo would have been equally ridiculous, anything would have. She was as naked as Eve, her blue jeans gone, Till's sweater jettisoned, her underthings torn from her at some indefinite point in the shifting momentum of her battle against the current and the waves and the sucking rasp of the shingle. When she touched herself, when she brought her hands up to cover her nakedness, they were like two dead things, two fish laid out on a slab, and she fell to her knees in the dirt, hunched and shivering and looking round her with an animal's dull calculation.

In the next moment she rose and went round the corner of the house to the door at the front, thinking to clothe herself, thinking there must be something inside to cover up with, rags, a bedsheet, an old towel or fisherman's sweater. But what if there were people in there? What if there was a man? No man on this earth had seen her naked but for the doctor who'd delivered her and Till, and what would she say to Till if there was a man there to see her as she was now? She hesitated, uncertain of what to do. For a long moment she regarded the door in its stubborn inanimacy, a door made of planks nailed to a crosspiece, weather-scored and unrevealing. She tapped at the door, hoping to forestall anyone who might be lurking inside. Finally, she tried whispering "Hello? Is anybody home?"

There was no answer. She lifted the latch and pushed open the door to a rustle of movement, dark shapes inhabiting the corners, a spine-sprung book on the floor, shelves, cans, a sou'wester on a hook that made her catch her breath, fooled into thinking someone was standing there. It took a moment for her eyes to adjust, the shapes manifesting themselves all at once—furred, quick-footed, tails naked and indolently switching, a host of darkly shining eyes fastening on her without alarm or haste because she was the interloper here, the beggar, she was the one naked and washed up like so much trash—and she let out a low exclamation. Rats. But what were they doing here on an untamed island set out in the middle of the sea? Had they swum? Sprouted wings?

The thought came and went. She flapped her arms savagely. "Get out!" she shouted, rushing at them, whirling, clapping her hands. "Get!" They blinked at her—there must have been a dozen or more of them—and then, very slowly, as if it were an imposition, as if they were obeying only because in that moment her need was stronger than theirs, they crept back into their holes. But she was frantic now, snatching the blanket up off the cot without a thought for the rattling dried feces that fell like shot to the floor and wrapping it around her even as she fumbled through the cans on the shelf—peaches in syrup, Boston baked beans, creamed corn—and the utensils tossed helter-skelter in a chipped enamel dishpan set on the counter.

She ate standing. First the peaches, the soothing thick syrup better than anything she'd ever tasted—syrup to lick from the spoon and then from her fingertips, one after the other—then the creamed corn, spooned up out of the can in its essential sweetness, and then, finally, a can of tuna for the feel of it between her teeth. Only when she was sated did she take the time to look around her. The empty cans, evidence of her crime—theft, breaking and entering—lay at her feet. She sank down on the cot, pulling the rough blanket tight round her throat, and saw, with a kind of restrained interest, that the walls were papered over with full sheets torn from magazines, from *Life* and *Look* and the Sunday rotogravure. Pinups gazed back at her, men perched on tanks, Barbara Stanwyck astride a horse. A man lived here, she decided, a man lived here alone. A hermit. A fisherman. Someone shy of women, with whiskers like in the old photos of her grandfather's time.

She found his clothes in the trunk in the corner. Two white shirts, size small, a blue woolen sweater with red piping, and a stained and patched pair of gabardine trousers. Without thinking twice—she'd pay him back ten times over when they came to rescue her—she slipped into the trousers and the less homely of the two shirts and then stepped back outside to see if she could find him or one of the men who lived in the other shacks, because if there were four shacks there must have been four men. At least. And now, standing outside the door with her face turned to the nearest shack, some hundred feet away, she did, in fact, call out "Yoo-hoo!"

No one answered. The only sounds were the ones she'd become inured to: the sifting of the wind, the slap and roll of the breakers, the strained high-flown cries of the birds. She went to each of the shacks in succession, and though she found signs of recent habitation—a bin of rat-gnawed potatoes, a candle melted into a saucer, more canned goods, crackers gone stale in a tin, fishing gear, lobster traps, two jugs of red wine, and what might once have been sherry turning black in an unmarked bottle beneath a float of scum—she didn't find anyone at home. It was as if she were one of the wandering orphans of a fairy tale arrived in some magical realm where all the inhabitants had been put under a spell, turned to trees or animals—to rats, black rats with no fear of humans. Finally she went back to the first shack, opened another can of peaches, ate them slowly, one by one, the juice running down her chin, then stretched out on the cot, wrapped herself in the blanket, and slept.

Beverly woke to the declining light and creeping chill of evening. She sat up with a start, uncertain of where she was, and there were the rats, gathered round, staring at her. They were leisurely, content, taking their ease, draped over the chair pulled up to the counter, nestled in the refuse on the floor, hunched over their working hands and the things they'd stolen to eat. Enraged suddenly, she shoved herself violently from the bed and went out the door, muttering to herself, letting out a string of obscenities she never until that moment realized she knew, and began tearing through the heap of driftwood stacked behind the shack. Without thinking, without regard for her unprotected hands or the sobs rising in her throat, she flung one log after another over her shoulder and onto the flat between the shacks. When all of it was heaped in a towering pyre, she got newspaper, rat-shredded, from a cardboard box just inside the door of the second shack. The matches she found in a jar atop the woodstove.

She waited till it was full dark, hunched over her knees in the too-tight shirt and the blue sweater with the red piping that smelled of a strange man's sweat, eating pork and beans from the can and savoring each morsel, before she lit her signal fire. And when she lit it and fed it and kept on feeding it, the flames rose thirty feet in the air, visible all the way to the mainland she could just make out through the gauze of fog as a series of drifting unsteady lights, as if the stars had fallen into the sea. The fire raged, sparked, tore open the night. Someone would see it, she told herself, someone was sure to see it. That first night she even called out at intervals, a hollow shrill gargle of sound that was meant to pierce the fog, ride out over the sea and strike the hull of whatever boat might be passing in the night to see her fire and hear her call. The second night she saved her breath. By the third night she'd used up nearly all the wood she could scavenge and thought of setting the shacks afire—or the chaparral. At the end of the first week, she was resigned. She scattered rats, ate from the cans, drank from the barrel. When she wasn't gathering wood she lay in bed, dozing, thumbing through the yellowed newspapers to weigh the news of events that had been decided years ago, politics, economics, war stories, and would the Allies take Monte Cassino and push through to Rome, would the Marines land at Guadalcanal, would Tojo triumph or turn his sword on his own yellow belly?

Her fires, of necessity, were smaller, but beacons nonetheless, urgent smoldering pleas for help, for release. She saw boats suspended in the distance with their tiny quavering sails and she waved her arms like a cheerleader, fashioned flags from sticks and the tatters of an old faded-to-pink towel and waved them, too, but the boats never grew larger or drifted out of frame, as static as figures on a canvas tacked to the very farthest wall in the most enormous room in the world. No one came. No one landed. No one existed. And where was Till? Where *was* he? He would have come for her by now, if he was alive, and how could he possibly have died in America, aboard his own boat off the lobster-rich Channel Islands, when the Japs hadn't been able to sink him in the whole wide blinding expanse of the Pacific?

The answer was too hard to grasp so she let it go. She let it all go. And then, on the first day of what would have been the third week of her imprisonment in a place she'd come to loathe in its changeless, ceaseless, ongoing and never-ending placidity and indifference and sheer brainless endurance, a Coast Guard cutter, free as a cloud, rounded the point and motored into the cove.

And what did the Coast Guard find? A sunburned woman unused to the sound of her own voice, her hair stringy and flat and her eyes focused on nothing. She was the wife of a drowned man, a widow, that was all. She climbed into the rowboat and the sea shifted beneath her and kept on shifting until the big boat, the cutter, sliced across the channel under the downpouring sun, until the shore, with its sharply etched houses, swaying palms, and glinting automobiles, rose up to take her in and hold her as firmly and securely as she could ever hope to be held again.

YOUR BIGGEST FAN

by MONA AWAD

YOU'VE JUST POLISHED off a mickey of vodka, seven kamikazes, and six dirty mothers. It's getting to be around that time of night, that hour, when you feel you ought to call your biggest fan—the fat girl.

Now even though it's Friday night and very, very late, you know the fat girl will be home. The fat girl is always home. Likely as you last left her. Wearing a frilly white nightgown. In the process of making something like muffins. Waiting for your call.

And you are right. She is ridiculously happy to hear from you, as usual—another undeniable plus about the fat girl. In this regard, she is so unlike Some People, who too often hang up upon hearing your voice, or let the phone ring and ring when you know damn well they're home. No—the fat girl actually gasps when she learns it's you. You can even hear how her plump little mouth forms into a quivering red O of surprise. "Oh my gosh! Oh my gosh!" gushes the fat girl. Because she is just so excited! Because she just can't believe you called!

You say you hope you aren't calling her too late, even though you know you are not. You could never call the fat girl too late.

"No, no!" she cries. "Not too late not too late!" She is just *so glad* to hear from you. "I was getting a little worried, actually," she admits.

It's sweet how the fat girl worries. She really cares, unlike Some People, who have told you point blank, just tonight, that it doesn't matter to them whether you live or die.

Well, you've had a hell of a day, you tell the fat girl. A hell of a day. "Mind if I come over?" you ask her, even though you already know she never minds, and that, in fact, she was sort of hoping you might.

Now, it's been a while since you paid a visit to the fat girl. It's been a while since you fishtailed your way through a dark night of the soul to crash and burn against one of her front-lawn garden gnomes. It's been a while since you staggered up her steps, collapsed onto her WIPE YOUR PAWS! welcome mat, made her wicker wreath rattle by banging and banging your head on her front door. You haven't been to see her, in fact, since your last crisis, wherein you lay on her couch all night, drinking all her strawberry wine and then some, while she nodded sympathetically and made you fudge.

Tonight, as you careen down her daffodil-flanked walkway, you are pleased to find things as you left them. There is the swaying yellow square of light that is her front window. There are the carefully clipped rose bushes you once retched in. There are her window boxes full of fussy little purple flowers you can't help but finger, giggling. There is the fat girl filling the doorframe: her cheeks flushed, her eyes bright, a batter-covered spatula in her hand, cooing come in, come in, come in.

Some People can't even be bothered to throw an extra Pop-Tart into the toaster when you come over. The fat girl, on the other hand, has lit all of her vanilla-fig-scented candles in anticipation of your arrival. She has refilled her whimsically shaped potpourri bowls with Holiday Spice. She is bent over the oven right now, hands swathed in chef-hat-shaped mittens, praying aloud that you like Banana-Rama bread.

"Luvit," you tell the fat girl, and collapse onto her frilly couch, making all her hand-embroidered cushions crackle and hiss.

How it warms your heart to watch her waddle to and from the kitchen, bearing trays of things she knows you love: pigs in a blanket, rocky-road fudge bars, bologna and cheese sandwich triangles without the crusts—you hate the crusts, the fat girl knows and remembers, unlike Some People, who do not care to know or remember.

"I would have made more," she coos, "if I'd known you were coming." Next time maybe let her know just a little bit earlier? Just so she can be better prepared?

"Sure," you assure the fat girl. "Hey, you got anything to drink?" After the day you've had, you sure could use something stiff. Hell of a day, you tell her.

"Tell me, tell me," coos the fat girl, pouring you the last of her Lappish Hag's Love Potion, which is the only liquor of hers you didn't polish off the last time you were there.

"It's just... no one listens, you know?" you tell her. No one *really listens*. Especially not Some People, you say, as you take the chilled goblet from her plump, pink hand.

Now, the fat girl knows very well whom you mean by Some People. She *hates* Some People. In fact, even the mention of Some People makes her Betty Boop eyes go black and flinty.

"*I* listen," says the fat girl.

"You listen," you tell her. "Love how you listen," you say, giving her a wobbly smile and a wink that makes red blotches bloom all over her neck and chest. "S'matterofact," you tell the fat girl, reaching over and fiddling with the little blue bow nestled in the lace above her breasts, "s'one of the reasons I came over." You have a new set of songs you composed, and you would like the fat girl to be the first to hear them. "Furst," you assure her, holding up two fingers.

"Really?!" she cries, and claps and claps her hands. Oh! Oh! How you have made her night no her week no her month no her year!

How different her reaction—the reaction of the fat girl—from Some People's, who only rolled their eyes and muttered "Here we go" when you offered to play your new collection (tentatively titled *Novembral Musings*). Who filed their nails and frowned through whole tracks into which you squeezed out every last bit of your soul like drips from a well-wrung rag. Your biggest fan, the fat girl—she *listens*. She bites her lower lip in order to keep, you must assume, from crying. She hugs her fat arms, closes her eyes, and sways to the dissonant chimes and the atonal variations.

"Wow," is her first word. Wow, wow, wow, breathes the fat girl, pressing a chubby hand to her red-blotched chest. And when you ask if she'd like to hear more, she does not roll her eyes and say "Christ, there's more?" like Some People. "*Would* I?" cries the fat girl, like you even had to ask.

Epic. Primordial. Gritty. Incandescent. These are just a few of the adjectives the fat girl feeds you along with her Banana-Rama bread, her bologna and cheese triangles, her rocky road. She doesn't tell you not to quit your day job, like Some People. Instead she counsels, tears filling her eyes, never to give up. "Never give up. That's always been my motto," she says now, brushing Banana-Rama crumbs from her ruffled chest, her eyes wet, dark and adoring as a dog's.

You lay your head in the crackling white lap of the fat girl. You tell her how it's difficult *not* to give up... when there are Some People who don't appreciate you.

"But *I* appreciate you," she chimes, running plump fingers softly through your thinning brown hair.

"Well, Some People don't," you tell the fat girl; she gasps, all shock and indignation.

"Well, *Some People* have terrible taste," she sniffs, which is what you thought all along. It's amazing how you and the fat girl always seem to think the same thoughts at the same time. Like you share two halves of the same brain, you tell her. And she agrees.

"Like we're kindred spirits or something," she whispers, lowering her eyes. And then, after a moment, she looks up at you again.

"I wrote something," says the fat girl shyly. "For you," she adds. She wasn't going to read it before, but she feels it might go with the creative intent of track 8. She wonders if you'd like to hear it.

"Sure," you tell her.

You do not hear the elegy of the fat girl, which she reads in a quavering voice from a journal patterned with prancing fairies. You are too busy watching her, being transfixed. How her hands tremble, how the red blotches on her cheeks and chest bloom bigger and brighter (you make her so nervous!), how she peers shyly up at you from time to time through a curtain of dark hair, her eyes moony and bright. And you don't know what it is, if it's the dirty mothers or the vodka or her bad blueberry wine or some sort of black magic, but you can't take your eyes off the fat girl; she has transformed, as she always seems to do at around this time of night, into something you could almost love for an hour.

"S'great," you tell the fat girl, before she is even done, but it shuts her up. "*Yurr* great," you tell her, as you brush a lock of black hair away from her flushed cheek. Delicious, how she shivers at your touch.

"Oh," she whispers, and only hopes you won't forget her when you're famous.

"Won't," you assure her. How could you ever forget the fat girl? She is, after all, your biggest fan by far. And no one ever forgets their biggest fan. It's just bad manners. "Bad, bad, bad," you breathe into the hot, crimson ear of the shuddering fat girl.

By now all the vanilla-fig candles have burned down to their wicks. And all the sandwich triangles and fudge bars and Banana-Rama bread slices have been eaten, washed down with the last of her love potion. And you are dancing with all three of the fat girl to the best of your B-sides. You weren't going to play them at first, but she begged you to; she pressed the fleshy palms of her hands together and begged. Well, all right, fat girl.

Your hands, possessed by the wine, or so you tell yourself, run up and down her squishy sides, from her astonishingly firm breasts to the monstrous curves of her many flanks and thighs.

"Wrotethishsongbout you," you tell her, even though you are so far gone now you do not even know which song is playing, and whichever it is, you probably wrote it about Some People, their red lips and white limbs and wiles. Ah, but Some People, or so you feel now, does not deserve you or your music. In fact, you tell the fat girl, you are thinking of ending it with Some People.

"Really, *really*?" she squeals, like you have just told her this is one bow-strung puppy she can keep.

"Yup," you breathe into her warm, doughy neck, marveling at how, with one mere breath, you can make a whole fat girl tremble like a leaf.

Was it you who lowered the lights? Was it you who dragged her by the hair up the stairs and down the hall to the stuffed-animal-cluttered cave of her bedroom? All you know is the hammering of your own heart in the morning, the laughter of God ringing in your ears, when you wake up naked under her penguin-patterned quilt, your mouth still full of her long dark hair.

On a sheet of her Dancing Cats! stationery, you tell her you've made a terrible mistake. You don't know what you were thinking.

Probably you have a drinking problem, or maybe it's something to do with self-esteem—anyway you hope she understands. Though it's a fine note, it doesn't feel like enough. So you leave her an autographed copy of *Novembral Musings* (tentatively titled), which you hastily sign *To my biggest fan.*

It is only as you drive home, still drunk, through the dishwater-colored dawn, not stopping at stop signs, blazing through red lights, that you realize it was a poor choice of words. *Number-one fan*, you should have put. Of course, it's too late now.

Some People is waiting at your doorstep, tapping her witch-toed boot, drumming her fingers on her narrow white hips, frowning at you through curtains of long, layered red hair. She takes one look at the potpourri in your collar, the cat hair on your clothes, breathes your Banana-Rama-and-flesh scent, and knows where you have been and what you have done. "Despicable," she hisses. "Disgusting. With her?! I can't even believe it!"

And if your mouth weren't so full of cotton, if your throat weren't so parched from all that fat-girl wine, you would have said—Neither can I. Neither can I.

A week later, alone, alone in your basement apartment, the fat girl still won't take your calls. You leave message after message—mainly drunken, but sometimes sober—wait for her to call you right back, can't believe that she doesn't. It is only when you see her front window abruptly darken as you tipsily turn into her driveway one night that you understand that there has been no mistake.

Three weeks after that you're paying your first non-drunk visit to the fat girl. You don't know why. You only know you need to see her. You even left her a message earlier, saying you'd be stopping by and when, giving her that advanced notice. It's the only time you've ever been to see her dry, or during the day, for that matter, and the house seems different somehow. Smaller. Not swaying. Less-lethal lawn ornaments.

As you approach her door, wondering what the hell you're doing here and what you're going to say, you hear *Novembral Musings* wafting out of her half-open window. And though it comes as no surprise that she'd be playing it, your heart breaks. It breaks for the fat girl. Christ, she's loyal. Even when you gave up on her, she never gave up on you. It's enough to make you want to marry her. At least for a moment, in your mind.

Standing on the doormat, you knock a gentle knock. You knock and knock until the multi-seasonal wreath tumbles to the ground and still no answer. But you do not give up. After all, she never gave up on you. You go around back, hunch down in her hydrangea beds, and peer into her half-open window.

She's sitting on the couch with a slightly plump girl whom you vaguely recognize as her roommate. (You knew her mostly as a narrowed green eye that appeared and then disappeared in the crack of an upstairs doorframe whenever you came over.) Your album is blaring in the background. The girls are sharing a bottle of wine, laughing hysterically. The other girl is laughing so hard that she drops her wine glass, slides off the couch, and rolls onto the floor.

"Enough, enough!" she cries, flailing her arms in the air. "Turn it off! My stomach hurts! I can't breathe!"

You watch your biggest fan, the fat girl, reach for the remote.

"That," gasps the roommate, still lying on the floor, "was *the* funniest thing I've ever heard."

"Tell me about it," says the fat girl, in a voice you've never heard before; it has an edge, a sharpness you thought only lived in the voice of Some People. "You have no idea how hard it was for me to keep a straight face."

"I wouldn't have been able to," guffaws the roommate, wiping her eyes.

The fat girl, your fat girl, shakes her head. "Can you believe I actually told him it was good? That's what I hate. That's what I hate most. About *myself*," she says, in this alien voice. She presses the pads of her fingers to her temples; she closes her eyes and shakes her head again like she's trying to shake herself out of a bad dream.

"God, I was desperate," she sighs. "Pathetic. Pitiful."

"Can you please, please make me a copy?" pleads the other girl. "I could use a good laugh now and then."

"Sure," answers the fat girl, flicking her eyes at you and smirking. "I'll even *sign* it for you."

And then they both burst into laughter again, terrible, monstrous cackles that ring in your ears long after you've stumbled out of all her flowers and found your way home.

105 RIPARIAN LANE

by PETER ORNER

HE IS THINKING OF the downstairs bathroom in his father's house, the tiny bathroom they always referred to as the Powder Room. In his father's house, the house Popper grew up in until they fled—not at night, during the day, they ran away in the broad day. The three of them in the gravel driveway packing up his mother's VW bug with the last of their clothes and their junk and their pillows. His brother Leo put the top down so there'd be more room and the two of them sprawled on top of it all like the Beverly Hillbillies, trying to keep socks from blowing away in the wind. It was November. *Goodbye, house*, Miriam called. *Goodbye driveway, goodbye lawn, goodbye garbage cans, goodbye raccoons. So long, basketball hoop.* His mother drove with the cat in her lap, the cat screaming. They vagabonded to an apartment seven blocks away.

That was them leaving, but today the ecstasy of mutiny is long over, finished, history—today is an every other Wednesday and Popper is back, as per the divorce decree, in this house that used to be his house. Leo, being older, is exempt from any judge's orders. He can come and go as he pleases, and mostly he doesn't come to go at all. I'm through with 105 Riparian Lane, Leo says. So Popper's alone. His father isn't home from work yet. And he is in the Powder Room because it has a lock on the door and is a good place to smack off in private. Above the toilet is a small framed picture of a young pinkish girl. Under her chest, which is ruffly and flouncy and also pink, are the words *A Tribute to My Pretty Star*. Popper thinks, I'll give you a tribute, honeybaby. Only thing he's ever been early for. Let the experts call it pubertal; to him it's a siege. He's a pimpled doughboy in the muddy trenches of lust. He is—say it—battle-hardened. He can't appease himself fast enough, enough times, and his Pretty Star is his pretty savior. His father's porn has nothing on her. Her porcelain face, her fat, fat cheeks. Popper thanks his comrade to this day. As far as he knows she's still hanging above the toilet, wondering where he disappeared to. Where has he disappeared to?

But there was something else about the Powder Room other than the lock and his love. If you stood on the toilet itself you could see out a small window that had an excellent view of the Yarmos' driveway next door to the south. The Yarmos had a daughter about Popper's age. Her name was Daphne. He'd never known her very well because she went to private school and held herself aloof. Also, adding to her novelty was the fact that she'd been adopted, not as a baby but as a five-year-old girl. This gave her an air of independence, and Popper who was saddled with the knowledge that the rancor between his mother and father had created him had always been jealous of her. That Daphne could with a flip of her hand say, "Hey, you see those two over there masquerading as parents, *my* parents? No relation, none." To be able to cast off this town, this neighborhood, this street—it was a kind of awesome power. Even her name was incongruent. It was made up, like Yugoslavia. There was no Daphne Yarmo. Daphne Yarmo is fiction. And some days in spring she comes home from her private school in Lake Forest and lies in the driveway in her tweed private school field hockey–looking dress and stares at the sky and he standing on the toilet redirects all field operations toward imagining her skirt crawling higher and higher, exposing milky private-school thighs. Daphne Yarmo composing poems in her head on the asphalt driveway and Popper is a scumbag.

This happened so long ago. Daphne is enjoying her life somewhere, a productive life. Maybe she is an accountant, or a China specialist. Maybe she's a masseuse. He has no idea. After they moved away (a moving away that wasn't) he never once spoke to her, and the Yarmos themselves moved away in '87. She remains as static in Popper's mind as his Pretty Star. And here he sits in the middle of a Thursday in Chicago, in the Harold Washington Memorial Library, in the middle of a working Thursday, aimlessly opening and closing Dostoevsky and sickly conjuring thirteen-year-old pucky knees. Harold Washington himself would throw him the hell out of here. *I'm a sick man. I'm a wicked man. I am an unattractive man. I think my liver hurts.* And why is it that memory recedes but shame never stops bleeding? The whole world knows he's standing on the toilet aching himself to Daphne Yarmo. His father's emptied house, his furious hysterical loneliness, his nose against the pane, fogging it up. Only our disgraces are permanent. Once—only once—Daphne grabbed her ankle and raised her leg so that her foot was directly above her head and he was so stunned he stopped panting. That tweed dress collapsing over her face like a parachute. Everything in his life he's seen since has paled in comparison.

CONVERSATIONS WITH GIRLS

by SEAN CASEY

GROGAN WAS THE FIRST kid in town to have one. He was in the seventh grade, and an assortment of attractive hairs grew above his lip. Of course, when he was in the seventh grade, we were all in the seventh grade.

"How big?" we asked.

"Eight, nine feet," Grogan said.

"Where'd you get her?"

"Pond."

"What'd she look like?"

"Like a real nice individual. Superb upper-body strength."

"Awesome," I said.

"Inspiring," someone else said.

"I know," Grogan said.

After the pond experience, Grogan had conversations all the time. Mutual friend Neal Scoones told me Grogan had a full-lengther while skiing, hard to do given the loud sounds skis make, the air rushing past, and the garments covering ears and mouths. Also dangerous due to the high speeds.

"Grogan pulled it off," Scoones said. "They talked about a wide array of subjects, including sports."

Grogan had universally handsome attributes. There were those lip hairs of no small number, grown since early in the fifth grade—mature, fluffy, evenly spread. His two shapely eyes were positioned close enough to be regarded as one.

We voiced our wishes to Grogan. We wanted a whole girl, too. Grogan smiled the smile of unlimited knowledge.

"You dopes wouldn't know what to do with one," he said. "Especially a whole one."

Grogan, Scoones, and I grew up in a town that didn't have girls until the early '80s. Even after the girls arrived it was difficult for inhabitants to talk to them, let alone develop talk into a conversation. I'm saying this to make clear that I was in no way strange for not having plentiful conversations with girls. I was one of an unashamed many. Scoones, for one, was another.

When the girls were delivered—or, as some say, "traveled here of their own accord," which is not true, because I saw it, and they arrived on flatbeds—when the girls were delivered, I was young and uninterested. Avocado, our family dog, howled at the trucks, which deposited them in the lot behind The Ground Round. From there the girls quickly scattered to avoid the advances of business professionals.

At a certain point, though, and I'm not going to tell you when,

I grew of age. I had had several successful full-contact male conversations. I was ready for what was next.

The morning I made the decision, I was talking about all sorts of things with Will Nelson at the park. Twenty yards away Grogan appeared, walking with a young woman approximately twenty feet in height. Will and I stopped our wide-ranging conversation to watch theirs. Grogan stood beneath his girl like a man beneath a maple. Like many of his preferred interlocutors, she had extraordinary quadriceps. I couldn't hear what was said, but it had a lot of visual nuance and likely covered a galaxy of topics. It was clear when their conversation wrapped up. The girl threw Grogan into the gazebo. She beat feet. We felt her footsteps as she disappeared behind Town Hall.

I ran over to Grogan and helped him to stand.

"Grogan," I exclaimed. "Teach me!"

Grogan wiped blood from his forehead.

"Easy, Sullivan," he said. "Let's go buy me some Band-Aids."

At the drugstore, I told Grogan I was of age. I was ready.

"You haven't had your first?" he asked.

"Come on, Grogan," I said. "It's not easy. But look—" I jutted my upper lip. He squinted.

"You've got the requisite hair," Grogan said. "And the standard proportions. The obvious appendages are strong. Your eyes aren't contiguous, but they're close enough to see the truth."

"I should be able to have a conversation, Grogan. I've been drinking more than the recommended volumes of milk."

Grogan hammered at his knee to pop the cap back in place.

"Sure, Sully. But what you witnessed there—that wide-ranging conversation? It explored subject matter I knew nothing about.

I was unprepared for its many turns. I lacked interest in both topic and partner."

"You sure looked interested," I said. "Informed, too."

"Sure I did," he said.

The more he talked, the less ready I felt. I looked around. I lowered my voice.

"Grogan," I said, "I'm not sure I'll succeed, but I sure want to try. Will you prepare me?"

"No, I won't. And not because I don't deeply care about you, Sullivan. It's that success does not proceed from preparation. Conversation comes from the deepest, truest recesses of who in your case is Mike Sullivan. One flirts with the nervous, digestive, and endocrine systems."

I bought Band-Aids.

"I'm going to need ice, too," he said.

I bought ice. In the parking lot, he wrapped the bag of ice in his T-shirt, held it on his enlarged, purple knee, and continued.

"Have a conversation with yourself, Sullivan. Ask yourself, 'What type of girl does Mike Sullivan want?'"

Grogan was trying my patience. Sometime an expert like Grogan is so accustomed to ease in his area of expertise, he assumes that ease is freely available to others, instead of being the fruit of practice and handsomeness.

"Look at me, Grogan. Do I look selective?"

"Looks are secondary, Sully. If you go after any old girl, you'll find one who's going after any old guy. You're not one of those, are you?"

"I suppose not."

"You quaff the recommended volumes, avoid clothing with words on it, consider deeply the big questions. You prepare for a conversation that cracks the surface. Not one about weather and car tires."

"Damn right."

"Don't forget anatomy. In our longing for substantive conversation, sometimes we men overlook physical appearance. There's an accounting of physicality to consider. Height, depth, appendage count, ego width, circumference of knees. Stats don't necessarily ensure a conversation, but they never hurt it. Of course, there's also male finesse. Me? I can have a mutually affirming conversation with a girl even if she's got knees like harvest moons."

I didn't want to hear about any more of his successes. I told him I had things on my mind that required a sophisticated, sensitive female listener.

"Sensitive, Sullivan?" Grogan asked. "That large Barbara bruised some ribs."

I held out my arm and Grogan took it. As he limped and I walked slowly about town, I recounted my efforts. My conversations were like my attempts to flip off a diving board: I stood at board's end and looked out over the water. The kids below spoke at increasingly louder volumes. Body temperature rose.

"Follow me into these bushes," Grogan said.

We crouched behind potted shrubs in front of the drug store. The shrubs in no way concealed us. In fact, we made our presence more widely known by hiding. I expressed my concern that someone might see us. Grogan passed wind.

It wasn't long before a girl came into view. She made a stealthy approach. Though it was midday and shadows were short, she clung to slivers of darkness. Even at a height of fourteen feet, she was nearly successful in concealing herself. It took Grogan's pointing for me to find her.

"By the kiosk. A Red-Haired Beverly. Bipedal. Extremely rare."

Despite his injury, Grogan rose and dashed in an arc toward this purported Beverly, who, to my surprise, dashed in a similar arc toward him. Their approaches were not direct. Each missed the other by a good ten feet, then spun and returned.

Another, closer, miss. Grogan managed commentary between labored breaths.

"Mating sprints, Sullivan. Simultaneous chase and evasion."

They repeated the process several times, each time cutting the distance between them. At last, each ran straight for the other.

Instead of collision, a conversation ensued.

Grogan hummed exclamations.

"Mmmmnnnn! Hmnnnnnnn! Ermhhhhhhhh!"

He gesticulated boldly with appendages. Beverly opened her mouth and let fly a torrent of long ones.

"Eeeeeeiiiiiiiyooyooyoooooooooooayyyyyyyyyy!"

She worked arms and legs in flying corkscrews. She leapt without subtlety.

The conversation sure didn't sound mutually affirming. Instead of back and forth, its two parts were simultaneous. Each overlapped the other without consideration.

Abruptly, Grogan and Beverly halted again, and then began running back around each other. The circle unwound, larger and larger in diameter, until Grogan and Beverly were back where they started. Beverly made for the shadow she had left. Grogan sighed.

"What a bore!" he said. "Could you tell how badly I wanted out of that?"

I admitted to Grogan that I hadn't followed the conversation.

"Are you kidding? I have never heard a duller description of weekend plans." He sighed. "It's not all substantive dialogue, Sully. Not all girls are prepared to go deep."

* * *

Grogan said it was time to practice greetings.

"Greetings?" I asked.

"If you're lucky," he said. "If you're really lucky, small talk."

Half of the pool was set off for laps. The other half was left for recreation. By the board stood some boys and a full-grown man.

"See that guy?" Grogan said, pointing to the man.

"Yeah?"

"Pervert."

"Pervert?"

"One at every free swim."

The pervert waved.

"And only one," Grogan said, waving back. "If there were two, one or both would leave, or they'd fight it out. They're territorial, perverts."

"I didn't know that," I said.

We walked to the diving area.

"Stand aside, boys," Grogan commanded. "Sully needs the board."

The kids did as instructed, but the pervert intervened.

"Hey there, fella," he said. "These kids have an orderly line formed. You can't just barge in."

"Silence, pervert," Grogan said. "Get up there, Sullivan."

The pervert made a noise of frustration and left to report Grogan. I stepped up to the board. I walked to its end and hesitantly bounced.

"Now stay there," Grogan said.

Grogan left. I stayed. A few curious elderly men stopped in lap lanes to stare at me. One watched while doing the sidestroke. In the back, the pervert complained to the lifeguard.

"Sully!"

It was Grogan—his voice, at least. I couldn't see him. My attention was occupied by an enormous figure now on the deck. A girl, mid-development. Eleven, twelve feet.

"Sully!"

I spotted him. He was hanging from the girl's neck. The girl did not appear to know him.

"Sully, look!" he yelled.

"Where'd you get her?" I asked.

"Membership services," he yelled. "Name's Enid. I can't control her much longer. Do something pretty off the board and get over here."

I had always hoped to attract girls with wit and subtlety. But here I was, at the end of a diving board, receiving the unfiltered attentions of Grogan, Enid, some elderly men, some boys, and a furious pervert. All waited with confusion and expectancy for my first act of display behavior. Everyone wanted action; I wanted complete paralysis. The compromise was not going to be impressive.

The compromise was not impressive.

I surfaced and swam over to Grogan and Enid.

"Don't worry, Sully," Grogan said. "She was too busy trying to buck me off to see it. It certainly wasn't a flip, but it..."

Grogan's voiced dropped from my attention. Enid. All eleven feet of Enid. And only five feet away. I had never been so close.

I climbed out of the pool. Grogan was struggling to keep his arms around Enid's impressively broad neck. He must have loosened his grip, because she palmed his head and tossed him into the lap lane. She turned to me. Her body language was reassuring. There were low leg sweeps, thunder grunts, overhead arm pumps.

Grogan surfaced.

"There," he said. "You've made acquaintance. Go for it. Do what you feel."

I did.

I swung my arms in overhead circles. I did energetic deep knee bends. Enid fanned her knees, puffed her cheeks, made gross noises. I bobbed my head for air apples. With powerful jazz hands, I reached for the rafters.

"Promising, Sullivan!" Grogan interjected. "I'm already jealous of the wildly interesting conversation you're about to have. Not only is this Enid obviously a tremendous conversationalist, she's got all the right parts. Two arms, two legs—everything."

Without my bidding, my lips began to move. They moved with an agility I had before attributed only to horses, to horse-lips. Enid did the same. Words weren't released, but there was a shared weight to our exhalations. I felt comfortable assuming something downright communicative was about to happen.

While it required my temporary involvement in a Boston Crab and more flotation devices than I would have wanted in mouth, Enid and I had a vigorous, challenging, symphonic dialogue. Any lingering trepidation was burned away by an icebreaker Enid proposed that combined gluteal exercise with ululations. We were off. We explored subjects far removed from comfort zones and areas of expertise. I hadn't known the depth of my knowledge of monetary policy or opera. I hadn't known a story of a cub-scout sleepover at the Museum of Science could make me weep and laugh in equal measure.

I only wish it had continued. In an unfortunate digression, the conversation slipped into informality. I inquired into road conditions, whether branches from a recent storm had been cleared. I asked whether her uncle, a truck owner, plowed during the winter. She took exception. She crouched low, as though tying her shoes, and rose with such force that she shot upward. She broke through the ceiling. She soared off in the direction of New Hampshire.

* * *

I've had conversations since with girls with deltoids of greater girth, and earned the admiration of Grogan and Grogan's mentor Tim Sidebottom, but no accomplishment has approximated this first encounter. It provided, in condensed form, a lesson I cannot exhaust. It took all of life's difficulties and shot them through with edification, joy, and a cardiovascular workout. It was not unlike swimming: I was suspended in space, in a medium that provided resistance but through which I could move, and in which, if I did nothing, I would die.

And it was not without pleasure for my reluctant conversation partner: even as she smashed through the ceiling of the YMCA that afternoon, Enid smiled. Grogan contended that it was a grimace, and that only the angle at which Enid flew made the expression look like a grin, but Grogan was jealous.

LETTERS FROM THE ACADEMY

by Tom Barbash

Dear Mr. Wilcox,

I would like to let you know how your son Lee is progressing at the Tennis Academy. I've chosen to communicate by letter because I believe what we're witnessing requires more than a casual phone call or email, as I suspect you will agree.

I should start by confessing that I did not at the outset peg Lee as much of a player. Your son was a bit spacey, and antisocial, really, whereas the main cadre of top players cling to one another like a pack of young wolves. Lee has a tendency to look away when you speak so that it appears he isn't listening, though it has been my experience, as I'm sure it has been yours, that he's heard every word. He has invariably incorporated everything I've suggested into his game.

By the second week I'd see him staying late in front of the backboard and hitting way into the night, and there again at dawn with a hopper of balls and the targets, practicing a thousand or more serves. And now, a month in, I can see just a little Becker in his volleys and a touch of Agassi in his returns. I do not use those terms lightly. In the last tournament Lee was made to play the fourth seed, a boy from Kentucky with a huge serve-and-volley game, and Lee destroyed him in straight sets—6–2, 6–2. He never brags about his accomplishments, but I figured Lee would have told you this; when I talked to him a few days afterward, though, I understood that he probably didn't. He said he hadn't spoken to you in a while.

Lee won two other matches in that tournament, and when he finally lost, it was because of a broken string that forced him to borrow a racket. I plan to make a deal with Wilson so that Lee can begin to receive free equipment. I hope this will be an arrangement you will go along with. There is nothing you would need to do financially, but Lee would have to wear only Wilson clothes and use only Wilson rackets. In all other respects, I now think, he is ready for the responsibility such a deal would entail.

He still reads all the time when he isn't practicing, and I wonder if that's what's caused his eyes to deteriorate. Usually he wears his contacts when he's playing, but sometimes he wears those thick glasses which makes other kids poke fun at him, although to his credit he doesn't seem to listen to them or care all that much. I'm not sure he has any real friends here, other than a boy from the school our athletes attend. This boy doesn't play tennis, but he watches Lee play, and smokes cigarettes, which I certainly hope Lee does not do, because it would result in his suspension from the Academy. So far, so good. There have been no issues with girls, although a few seem to be taking interest in him. I don't think it would be all that bad for Lee to go on a date or two, but I have not spoken to him about it, and I imagine that's more your territory than mine. There have been off-color things said about Lee and the boy from the school, although that's what's always said about unusual kids. I have caught Lee staring a few times at Vivi, the girl from Denmark, who is one of our best players, and is something to look at.

What is so remarkable about Lee is his ability to focus on a single task, so unusual for a boy his age, or for anyone at any age. The world recedes for Lee when he is on the court, and his face looks purposefully placid, like Borg's or Lendl's. It's rather intimidating, really. And he has a terrific sense of balance. As he runs you can imagine him keeping a stack of books over his head and not spilling one. His racket speed has improved, as has his footwork. These improvements are incremental, and barely detectable day to day, but I'm beginning to think he'll be one of our top players by this spring. It will be a different life for him, and perhaps for you, because I believe he will be traveling soon for tournaments, perhaps to the Nationals. And I for one would like to be part of that.

I think that tennis isn't really all that important to Lee, but that whatever is in front of him becomes important, and tennis has been in front of him. He has a remarkable memory, and seems to be able to read a book a night. I'm not sure I've ever seen him particularly upset, or all that happy, although when he's hanging out with the boy who smokes cigarettes and when he's watching Vivi play he becomes more animated. That is all I can tell you right now. I hope this is as exciting to you as it is to us at the Academy. We are expecting very big things from Lee.

Sincerely yours,
Maximillian Gross

My Dear Mr. Wilcox,

I fear you have been out of town and therefore unable to reply to my last letter, or else you've read it and may still respond. I wanted to fill you in on the progress since our last correspondence, if we can call it progress, and I think we can. Lee has been practicing even harder, working on his footwork and volleying. It has gotten so that five boys can strike shots at him nearly simultaneously and he will cleanly volley all five balls back. He can retrieve the deepest lob after nearly touching the net, then sprint back for a drop shot on the opposite side of the court. The player who comes to mind when he does this is Wilander, or maybe Borg, whose fitness was legendary.

Wilson has sent the first shipment of rackets, and I have strung them each with a combination of gut and synthetic nylon at fifty-two pounds, which allows for a tremendous amount of topspin but means that on flat shots Lee will still be able to keep the ball in the court.

The boy he hangs out with has lately taken to smoking a pipe and wearing an army cap. Lee's grades have been outstanding in all his classes except for public speaking, where he got a B-. At sixteen, he reads at the graduate-school level, and his vocabulary is that of a man twice his age.

I have signed Lee up for a series of satellite tournaments, which will bring him in front of some significant crowds and provide us with a good testing ground. I very rarely tell a parent that their son or daughter has what it takes to make a living at our sport, but in Lee's case it is becoming apparent to us all. Just last week a collegiate player from Florida Tech stopped by the Academy to train with Lee. At the end of the day they played a set and Lee thrashed him 6–1. It was only practice, and the collegiate player, one of our alums, was somewhat out of shape, due to a month-long spell of mononucleosis. But the margin of victory was what sent shockwaves through the Academy dining room that night.

I am concerned because we have not received your check for the spring, and while I'm quite confident that Lee will qualify for a full scholarship, I would like to talk to you about this and other matters, preferably on the telephone so there can be some back and forth. It would be better still if you could make the trip down here and see what your son's life is like. The other day I observed Lee and the Danish girl sitting on the practice court bench after a long workout, the two of them quite sweaty and flush, and I saw the Danish girl several times touching Lee's arm, and then resting her head on his shoulder. Again, I cannot be sure if there was anything significant going on, and nor would it be a problem, as the Danish girl is from a good family and is an extremely talented player ranked very high in Denmark. I only think that Lee would profit from some adult guidance on this matter.

The boy who smokes cigarettes is also a friend of the Danish girl. I saw him out on the court one night in blue jeans and the wrong shoes, hitting balls with Lee while the Danish girl watched. We have strict dress rules at the Academy, and strict rules about allowing guests to play without clearing them through Clara at the front desk. I spoke to Lee about this and he assured me the smoker would not be playing at the Academy again. The three of them ate together at a table at the side of the pool, pizza slices cribbed from the Academy pizza party. I did not see this as a problem, and would like Lee to feel he has freedom here and isn't being watched around the clock. There are entire days in which I barely see Lee, though not an hour passes without my thinking of something else we might do to optimize his prodigious talent.

There is a junior Davis Cup player coming to the Academy from Chile, a boy whose game harkens back to a young Yannick Noah, and I would like to have Lee play him in a match inside the newly refurbished Academy stadium. The match will be videotaped, and we will post clips of the most exciting points on the Academy website provided it goes well and Lee is successful, as I'm quite certain he will be.

With warm regards and in distant partnership,
Maximillian Gross

Dear Mr. Wilcox,

The match with Javier, the Chilean Junior, was more than my middle-aged heart could take. In the warm-ups Lee was relaxed, powdering his groundstrokes and crushing his overheads, and he took a 5–1 lead in the first set. But after that he began to spray shots, and double fault, like a pitcher who mysteriously and suddenly loses control. I have seen this sort of meltdown eight or nine times, but it usually occurs for boys with more volatile temperaments than Lee's. It might have served as a lesson had Lee in fact lost the match, but Javier had his own, more theatrical and sub-equatorial meltdown in the third set, and Lee won through attrition more than perseverance.

When the match was over Lee and the boy who smokes went to the movie theater at the mall. I saw them buy two pretzels, a slushy, and a chicken sandwich of suspect pedigree. They sat in the eighth row. I know this because I was in the fifteenth. It is not unusual for me to go to the movies, and I hadn't intended to spy on them, but the movie was at a convenient time for me, and I planned to leave before the end of the film so as not to inhibit them on their afternoon escape. There are no rules against seeing a movie on a Sunday, provided you make it back by dinnertime, and provided you've played at least four hours and run three miles, which Lee had done. I heard Lee laugh several times during the movie, once at a very serious and in fact poignant moment—a last conversation in a hospital ward between a husband and wife—and I'm quite sure he and the smoker were upsetting the family who sat in front of them.

The other boys at the Academy had a basketball tournament that night to which Lee declined participation and instead played cards with one of the groundskeepers in the groundskeeper shack. Money was involved and Lee apparently ended up on the short end. I don't think it was a disastrous defeat, perhaps $100, but I suspect that Lee has been paying the groundskeeper back with some of the Wilson equipment he has been receiving. The basketball game went on until after ten, and afterward the boys drank Gatorade together on the Academy porch. Lee was back in his room by then, reading or doing sit-ups. (I have tried to match him in his exercise routine and am up to 125 sit-ups and 100 push-ups a day, which is not bad I would say for a man of forty-four.)

Thank you for the quick note you sent, which I know was written during a particularly busy time for you. And in answer to your question, yes, there are several other coaches who work directly with Lee, and he is not being singled out for special treatment. But I must say that if he was it would be because he is not an ordinary adolescent, and not an ordinary talent.

I am considering banning the smoking boy from the Academy grounds, but am reluctant to do so because I fear Lee would flee like a hostage from a barricaded embassy. Mostly my time is spent scheduling more matches for Lee, and better practice partners. This weekend we will go to Boca Raton for a tournament at the Escondido Club. They have not seeded Lee, and have no idea what they are about to see. I know that wherever Mrs. Wilcox is, and I choose not to believe the rumors, she is beaming with pride right now, as you in your own way must be. Lately in his forehand I am seeing a little of Jim Courier in the two years he won the French, and in his footwork I have noticed an aspect of Gustavo Kuerten. I believe too that the Danish girl is now in love with Lee, as I saw her leaving a note outside his door the other night. I admit I did lift the note and thought of opening it, but did not. I relate this to you to indicate that I do not want to get in the way of Lee and his friendships.

I will write to you from the Escondido Club, undoubtedly with exciting news. There is a rumor that Sampras might stop in to watch a match or two. Wouldn't that be something?

Yours,
Maximillian Gross

Dearest Mr. Wilcox,

I am writing you from the veranda at the Escondido, which is filled with players and parents and coaches, much of South Florida's tennis aristocracy. Lee is one of four Academy players entered in the tournament, and from where I sit I can see him rallying with a junior player from Taiwan.

I'm happy to report that Pete Sampras is indeed staying at the Escondido, and was seen this morning at the breakfast buffet with his movie-star wife and their two sons. It is hard to see Sampras eating his eggs and oatmeal and sausages and not think of how many times on the brink of a Grand Slam he flamed out so impotently in the French. There is nothing sadder than seeing a big hitter stumble on slow clay.

I wonder how much of you is in Lee, and whether in your early days with the All City Orchestra and later with Stan Kenton and Lionel Hampton you were equally intense and abstracted. I must say that I've always loved your work. He told me yesterday about the first time he saw you perform, when he was eleven and you were in Montreal. I now own a dozen of your CDs and I play them in the morning when I awake and drink my coffee.

In the evenings Lee goes boogie boarding with Vivi, which I think is perfectly healthy, though I know some coaches might discourage such activities. In Lee's case I think we should welcome any broadening of his interests—moments in which he can be a kid, if you will.

As for our reason for being here, Lee did as well as we could have hoped. We played him up an age group, in the 18s, and he won his first three matches before losing to the second seed. Sampras watched four or five games of Lee's defeat, and said—these were his exact words—"this kid is pretty good." I wish you could have been there to hear that, but I hope you can imagine yourself where I was, hearing such a career-making compliment!

I was thinking of you, Mr. Wilcox, and what you might have done in this instance, how you would have responded. I was channeling the moment in the Frankfurt documentary where you take that pretentious journalist to task.

You bet your fucking ass he is, I said, though it is far from my nature to use that sort of language, and certainly not in front of the greatest champion in our sport. I may have said some other things to the hotel staff there, who warned me to be quiet. I was escorted to my room and asked to leave first thing in the morning.

The fuck I will, I thought.

I watched the end of Lee's match from my room. I thought the last match might go on forever. Do you know those rallies where each of you digs to the bottom and reaches his racket out and manages the strength to knock the ball across again, and then sprint on strained calves and cramping stomach back to the center of the court for more? Was it like that on those late nights when you played one last set at Birdland?

From where does genius arise?

When he lost, Lee shook the other boy's hand and then went down to the beach and watched the ocean for an hour or so. I joined him there, and after a while I brought him to one of the restaurants inside, where I bought him a fish dinner which he ate without a word.

"Would it be okay if I stopped playing for a while?" he asked me afterward.

"Why would you stop playing?"

"I feel tired," he said.

"Are we talking a few days? A week?"

"I don't know," he said. "Maybe more than a week."

"Whatever you need," I said. And then he collapsed.

There was a doctor in the hotel who said it was simply heat exhaustion and cramps. They told him to rest with a cold washcloth on his forehead, and to drink electrolytes. At around eleven he went downstairs with the Danish girl. They sat by the pool with their feet in the water. I watched them for a while and then went to bed.

In the morning Lee was on the court, hitting with Pete Sampras as though none of this had happened. I stood on the veranda with my suitcase packed, waiting for a taxi to come and take me to another hotel. Sampras kept staring over at me, unsmiling. May I say here that the champ has not aged terribly well? Not in his face anyhow. The sun has been particularly unkind to him, giving him the deep lines of an aging lifeguard. Nor has his hairline held up as he must have hoped.

When they'd concluded their workout, Sampras told me I should stay away from Lee. And that Lee would be traveling with Pete as his practice partner.

My face felt hot, and my jaw tightened.

"But you don't play tournaments anymore," I said.

And he said, "I know a bad situation when I see one."

An argument ensued, and I probably handled it badly, though I think the staff at the Escondido was equally to blame. As a result, my continued employment at the Academy is under discussion, and I have not seen or heard from Lee since then. While Pete Sampras is a well-known celebrity, I do not know if it is in your wishes for your son to be the hitting partner of the washed-up balding husband of a second-rate Hollywood starlet. I told him he would need your permission for us to let Lee go anywhere, and he said "It's been handled" without explaining what that meant.

I believe great things are in the future for all of us, provided we sort out these complications. Would you be able to come soon to Florida, or might you be able to meet with me where you are to discuss strategies? If you hear from Lee, can you tell him that we still have work to do?

I am waiting for your reply,
Maximillian Gross

Venerable Mr. Wilcox,

There is not much these days to say for loyalty, or for all the careers I've nurtured, or for the reputation I've developed over decades of playing and teaching and learning about the game. Around ten of the players stood up for me, as well as a few of the cafeteria staff, and Antonio from the pro shop. But then there were lies spoken by a few of the least reliable, those most likely to profit from my expulsion, those who would turn the Academy into nothing more than a way-station to the pros. Gone would be any learning, or staring up at the sky, or listening to music such as your own. Gone would be the role of the imagination, so much larger in the life of a great athlete than most educators ever recognize. Go study the neurochemistry of Năstase and Pannatta and Budge, and certainly Federer and the great McEnroe, and you will see so much of what you might see in the brains of Mozart or Degas or, from your world, Miles Davis. What if this side of those brains had never developed? It was my job, I always believed, to link the physical and the metaphysical. Now it will be repetitive drills and weight training.

I saw Lee after he'd cleared out of his dormitory suite. I had the sinking feeling one has when one has been lied about. At the same time he seemed as though he wanted something from me, something he couldn't articulate. Tropical storm clouds gathered above us.

Neither of us knew then about my impending dismissal, and I said nothing to him of my talk with the director. I gave him a signed copy of Brad Gilbert's book on match strategy, and enough string to last him through the summer.

"Did you steal this?" he asked me.

"Of course not. It's yours," I said.

"I'm all set on equipment," he said, the sky darkening. "But thanks for the book."

On the title page I'd written a warning about Sampras that I now wished I could erase. *Big serves are like big bustlines: nice to look at, but no guarantee of a person's character.*

Nothing else was said, because it started to pour. I wondered what one does here—shake hands, embrace? In some measurable way my heart was breaking. We stood across from each other awkwardly and then he walked away.

The Danish girl has quit the Academy, and has accompanied me on my trip north to see you. She is crazy about Lee, she says, and wants to meet you. I am devoting myself now to her training, and believe she has it in her to make a splash at the Australian this year. I am not fond of the way people look at us while we're on the road, and so for now we are pretending to be father and daughter, like James Mason and Sue Lyon. There is nothing untoward about our interactions, though on one occasion Vivi, frustrated I believe by her inability to contact Lee, pressed her not unremarkably soft lips against mine, something that startled me and that I told her definitively could not happen again.

In the evenings, while she watches her TV shows, I've taken to long drives in no particular direction. I simply veer toward the empty road. Sometimes I play your music and listen to my own thoughts, and other times I break into tears for no reason other than that it makes me feel, oddly, loved. I try and remember the good things, matches I've won, people I've helped, a dog I once rescued from the pound. I think of walking the grounds at Wimbledon on opening day and praying it wouldn't rain.

Lee has been playing regional tournaments in California. I know this because I have a former player out there who has sent me emails about Lee's results. While he is winning matches here and there, I have no doubt that his progress has stalled outside the Academy, and I wonder whether Pete Sampras has the time to devote to him or whether he's simply found a third-rate coach out there to feed Lee balls. I wonder if there's a library out there, or anyone to go to the movies with. I wonder what happened to his friendship with the boy who smoked pipes, whom I saw loitering around the Academy for a week or two after Lee left. I wonder about Lee's ability to so easily break his attachments, and whether that comes from the same place as your ability to end relationships with the women you have been with over the years, though I know I'm overstepping my ground here.

For the next week we will be staying at the Knights Inn in Kalamazoo, Michigan. There are courts nearby at the high school, and Vivi and I are at out there training. Are you available early next week? I would not mind at all making the trip to your house in Grosse Point.

With hopes of seeing you soon,
Maximillian Gross

Mr. Wilcox,

I imagine you are surprised to see the postmark on the outside envelope. But yes, in point of fact, I find myself living productively and gainfully in Copenhagen, Denmark, thanks to the efforts of Vivi and her parents, the Ingebritzens. They have put me up in an apartment outside their indoor tennis club, a mile or so from the great Tivoli Amusement Park. I am now coaching five young ladies and two young men, all of whom have some degree of talent, the best being Vivi. I read somewhere that you lived in this city for a year, and I wonder if there are any places you would have me go in my first months here. I did make it to your house, you know, though it must have been when you were in Los Angeles visiting with Lee and the Samprases. Did they have you to their ugly house? I find myself swinging these days from stretches of loneliness and doubt to pockets of unrestricted happiness, and as strange as it sounds I think I owe both of those moods to you. To your music, your imagination, and your strange and gifted son. If I never see him again he will still live within me, as do you, Mr. Wilcox. The Danish girl and I had a two-hundred-shot rally today, and one nearly as long right after. I'm wondering how many times early in your career you were in places like this, relying on your wits and your talent and a woman who did not judge you, who trusted you when you'd forgotten how to trust yourself. I do not often think of Lee these days, but I hope he is in your life where he belongs. As you requested, I will not write again or try to get in touch with you or Lee, but know that you will always be part of my neurochemistry, the part of me that sings and mourns and deeply understands. This is what I've learned from your music, and from my coaching, and what I will continue to pass on to the Danish boys and girls, of whose talent I am sole guardian.

I am taking a Danish immersion class at night, and now when I dream I dream in Danish. When I wake up in my Copenhagen apartment, under my cold cotton sheets, I sometimes feel touched by magic, as though nothing in my life can ever go wrong. Do you know this feeling? Did you feel it when you saw your son hitting peerless groundstrokes with the great Pete Sampras, and if you did, did you recognize the gift I'd given you?

Can we say that we are even?

Yours truly,
Maximillian Gross

DOES THIS LOOK FAMILIAR?

by DANIEL HANDLER

THERE MUST BE a way the world changes. The shop was farther from the inn than you might think, the miles hard to count on a winding road. They'd passed two cemeteries, maybe three, a mossy wall with boots waiting on top of it. You couldn't forget a thing like that. The way had been hilly but then opened up into fields of grass, or the stick figures of a vineyard in the off-season. The sun was always every which way—the visor in the car on the left-hand window, straight ahead, or useless. Of course the sun was moving, too, making nothing grow out of the plowed earth in another field, getting the berries fat and ripe on the bushes by the hairpin turn. There was only one road—you couldn't get lost—but you didn't know where anything was.

There was a small gravel square for parking. The couple was in their forties but paused with the car doors open, sandaled legs on the little stones—he sighed, she sighed—as if at their age it took longer to move, at their great age. Everything was air-conditioned, but it was angrily hot. These moments were hell—it was not showoffy to say so—with the blunt, stale air a long slap, slapping you down between the air-conditioned car and the air-conditioned shop. Hell, eight times this afternoon. Nine. Six. It was best to move quickly. They moved slowly.

Sleigh-bells on the doorknob—Ho ho ho! Someone is coming into the shop! Robin paused and let the air conditioning pat her down, but Glenn plowed right on through with just a glance at the inevitable roll-top desk where a woman sat smiling against a background of NO PUBLIC RESTROOM and her large, sweaty hair. He rounded a corner, down a little hallway like he'd been there before. Another set of sleigh-bells, dim. The woman from the shop glanced after him. It was a little shop.

"I guess he knows what he wants," she said, and Robin smiled at her purse and then at a basket with sets of colorful cotton napkins clothespinned together. Next to the basket were five bottles of barbecue sauce, one of them open, and a glass bowl of barbecue sauce, and a pint glass circling a haystack of frail breadsticks for dipping into the barbecue sauce. The surface of the sauce in the bowl was as flat as a poster. There must be places, new untouched territories like this, where no one has ever been.

Robin opened her eyes and smiled again. The basket and all this barbecue sauce sat on a pale blue table with a drawer in it and spindly little deer legs, like a nightstand for a guy who loves barbecue sauce and keeps his fingers clean with new napkins. Robin looked at the knob on the drawer, and the cloth sign reading DREAM hanging on the knob. They were not really antiquing, and this was not really an antique shop. Robin had bought a brooch maybe an hour up the road, at a shop full of old advertisements printed on tin: soap and liquor and Pepsi-Cola. There was nothing else to do but look at the shops. They'd have lunch at the next decent place that appeared. It wasn't a vacation, not really. Robin had gotten sick right before her last birthday, a virus or a bad shrimp, and this was the last weekend before the inn kept the deposit. It was almost her next birthday. They were here, enjoying themselves at the last minute, by force.

She took a step and looked at some rows of jam and a mute doll, and a shiny plank with old scissors nailed to it, scissors of bygone days splayed out like cheerleaders, not spelling anything. She tossed an "It's a beautiful shop" toward the desk and went to tell Glenn they could leave. The woman replied, "A very nice day." The hallway was shorter than it looked, with these drawings of flowers everyplace on the walls, the other sleigh-belled door there after a few steps. Through the glass Robin could see the garden with its tree and searing hot rocks, benches for sale and little spitting cupids. Glenn was on tiptoes, one foot perched on the head of a cinderblock so he could see into the top of a stout, very tall ceramic flowerpot. In the heat?

The sound was unmistakable. There must be a temptation—a small power that beckons changes into the world. There could be parts of the world that are more powerful in this respect, places of some uncommon magnetism. At the sleigh-bell sound Glenn zipped his fly and stumbled his foot off the cinderblock. It was so hot outside. Robin looked at him.

Glenn had been—*peeing* into the vase?

"It's not a vase. It's a flowerpot," Glenn said. He was sweaty, as unrepentant as a fork in the road. "I had to go someplace. No bathrooms anywhere we stop."

I had to go someplace. Robin looked down into the flowerpot. Glenn's pee eddied on the earthy bottom. Robin had once seen her husband blush at a joke her friend told—or was it when their old neighbor spit, a rough wet spit, onto the sidewalk? Anyway, he'd blushed. Early in their marriage he couldn't even listen to gossip, standing up abruptly at the table when a colleague got catty and clearing the dishes to down extra wine in the kitchen until it was over. *Unseemly*, was his word for it. Now they were, more or less, on vacation for the weekend. They had rented a Volvo to get to the inn, with printed directions and a map they didn't need. The woman from the shop had a breadstick in her mouth on their way out—was it speckled with sauce?—tinkling goodbye with her fingers. It was hell again until the car started and the air conditioning slowly came alive.

The restaurant entrance was a terrible mud room, useless in the heat and smelling like a Band-Aid, but then it opened out into a very nice place of dark wood and windows, where couples sat laughing with gin-and-tonics or iced tea, or sat quietly, heat-defeated, with gin-and-tonics or iced tea. Robin sat facing the door, making the scene in the garden uglier in her mind. She could see his hangy dick in her head, dripping the last of its rude errand as he zipped up, and hear the sloshing of his pee when the flowerpot bobbled, though none of these things had happened. They were farther down the road. She unrolled her napkin and reminded herself that it was done with. It had happened, yes, but it wasn't happening now. A salad now, a piece of fish. They would never see the shop again. After a silence in the car he'd muttered, finally, "Sorry, okay?" She put the tiny box on the table, the box she'd watched the lady tuck together at the other shop. Lunch now and a brooch, look at the brooch.

The waitress brought their wine and Robin took a tangy sip and looked at her husband. They'd been married fifteen years now. They had two children, a son starting high school and his sister, two years younger and almost taller. If they were here they'd be cranky, though they wouldn't have minded the heat. Glenn would read precisely from a guidebook—he was a surgeon, he'd invented a cleaner way of operating on someone's lungs—and the children would be rolling their eyes. Robin smiled and missed them, and then thought of them stepping into the garden, the sleigh-bell ringing, and Glenn, right in front of their eyes, pissing into a vase. "So where are you guys visiting us from?"

"Caesar salad with bay shrimp," said Glenn.

Robin told her where they were from. "We're staying at the inn up a ways."

"Down a ways," the waitress said with a smile.

"It's so hilly here," Robin said. "How can you tell?"

"Lived here all my life," she said. "Or since high school, anyway."

But she looked like a kid! Robin looked at Glenn, who was patting the empty pocket of his shirt. "Can I smoke here?" he asked. "What's the law here? Where am I?"

"You don't *smoke*," Robin said, but Glenn and the waitress laughed like they knew better than she did.

"Outside you can," the waitress said. "Ma'am, what about you?"

"You don't *smoke*," Robin said again, closing the menu. "I'll have the trout, I guess, with rice. You don't smoke!" she almost cried to her husband, whose hand had just crept out of its pocket and held, sure enough, no cigarettes. Glenn looked at her with narrow, gritty eyes, and Robin fell back down in the booth, sharply, as if he had really said it: *Leave me the fuck alone.*

"Trout with rice," said the waitress. Now *she* was blushing. On the table, next to the dried flower in the tiny ceramic cup, was a small pepper grinder, a salt cellar, and a clear glass bottle of barbecue sauce.

There must be a way. If you stretched your arm out and considered the way of the world, it would run down from your body someplace to the very tip of your fingertips, or the other way, up your arm to your shoulder to your lips like a sleazy, seductive kiss.

And so if the world changes on you, it is simply another person who is suddenly being seduced and romanced, and this should be no more surprising than a questionable lover shifting his tactics onto another object, leaving you panting alone as you unmuss your clothing and return to the party with your head held high so that no one suspects how thoroughly you have been undone. The world changes and that is all. But Robin finished her wine and realized, seeing the glass empty and the sun outside still blazing away, that this was stupid. It was scarcely a line of reasoning, is what it was. Glenn didn't smoke, and had even pinned the brooch to her shirt—all wrong together, but just, he told her, holding the shirt away from her flushing skin so he wouldn't pin her too, to see what the stones looked like near her eyes. She shut the box and chewed her lousy trout. She had always done well at school. If the way of the world was a pier, jutting out into the water—

She stood up and strode outside. Hell. Glenn was nowhere until she followed the wall of the building to a sort of alley of dumpsters, her sandals digging up gravel and dribbling it between her toes. She was shaking one pebble out, legs bent crazy like a flamingo, when Glenn stepped into sight laughing in a puff of smoke, agreeing with something that—"*Yes!*"—the waitress said.

"Glenn?"

"It *was* hard," Glenn said to the waitress, and took a long drag. "We had to knock on every door, or hire guys, anyway, to knock and say 'Is this you? No? Do you know him?' We could have done it with actors in one afternoon, but the company was all hot on real people. That's all they want now. A pro can struggle for work, but you, with a cute face, you could be in a commercial tomorrow."

The waitress showed Robin she saw how cheap and silly this kind of flattery was, but she smiled and said "But do you ever lose sleep over it? I couldn't do advertising. Working all day to sell sneakers to kids when you could be, I don't know, healing the world?"

"Naw," Glenn said, just like that: *Naw.*

"I mean, do you have kids? What do you tell your kids when they see that shit?"

Robin remembered to put her shoe back on. "Yes," she told the waitress. "We have kids."

"Not this weekend," Glenn said with a wink.

"How old?"

"Twins," Glenn said, as Robin said "Fourteen and twelve" and stopped herself. "Twin girls, but this weekend we're getting away from it." He flicked his cigarette elsewhere, and turned at last to his wife. "Ready?" he said, although his salad, Robin was pretty sure, still sat untouched at a booth inside and air conditioned. "Ready to go?"

They argued. They argued over the cigarettes—over the two he'd taken from the waitress's pack on the way out after they'd paid, the two that were tucked behind his ear—his *ear!*—as he drove. Over which way to turn out of the restaurant lot and whether or not they were going too fast, the wrong way or the right way, back to the inn or farther away. Over whatever he'd told that poor girl—"*Woman*," Glenn had corrected, out of nowhere—and over that nonsense about the twins. Robin asked him if this was something he did, something he did sometimes as a prank or for fun, and quietly remembered an innkeeper, looking distressed, when years ago she'd come down the wide staircase with her sweater—it was cold outside—into the lobby to go to dinner. And then quietly remembered that no, that was a scene from a movie. Harrison Ford lying to an innkeeper. Glenn didn't answer. He was not a prankster; how could he be, a doctor? *Malignant, just kidding*. She gave up for now. They had argued before and it was not worse, then or now, and always eventually it got to Glenn not answering. So this part of the world—the crook of the elbow, the briny creatures on the leg of the pier—was the same.

"Did we pass this?" Glenn said after a silence. Together they looked out at a field, lined with grass. There were three metal tanks of something looking hot in the heat.

"It was the other way," Robin said, not without triumph.

Glenn smiled wearily. "It was not the fucking other way."

"Jesus, Glenn," Robin said, and the Volvo made a hairpin turn past some blackberry bushes. "It could be. We could be wrong. I mean there's no fork or anything. The inn—"

The sun wasn't setting, but it was low enough that the visors were helpless. "I'm hungry," Glenn said.

"Well, you didn't have lunch."

"Don't start. Jesus, this doesn't look right. What's this?"

Someone had erected a tall, flat—what?—a sign or a screen, along with what looked like barbecue pits in haphazard rows, and little metal posts—a drive-in movie theater, all overgrown now with the vines of something, scraggly in the off-season. "Turn around," Robin said. Glenn turned around.

It could be that nothing beckons change, and here is where the infidelity of a lover is most familiar. There is no reason for so many times when the world shifts on you. Robin had never been unfaithful, but she had thought of it—of course she had—and the first time she'd thought of it the world, it was true, had curved, sharply and with wickedness, many years ago but permanently. Had it really been this long from the restaurant? There was no sign of the gravel driveway, just a church spire rising over some dense trees—something they never would have looked twice at—and a carved stump, alone in a grassy field. It had been made to look like an old man, or a gnome, maybe.

"Does this look familiar?" Glenn made another turn and Robin saw a pair of boots—bright, bright red—on top of a mossy stone wall. "Yes," she said. "We're on the right way." But then an ivy-covered billboard—ESUS SAVES, the J faded and half-vined in, made her shake her head and think the other boots had just been ordinary brown work shoes. You wouldn't forget a vineyard on a hill, a cemetery next to a vineyard—surely that would have prompted a joke. The wine throbbed in Robin's head. Nobody said anything.

At a white gas station they stopped. It looked like it had been painted yesterday, gleaming in the heat, and a much-too-big sign said FOOD GAS with a design that looked like an equal sign in the middle. Food equals gas. This was wrong. They would have joked about it.

"I'll get out," Robin said. Glenn nodded and took a cigarette from his ear. She could not think if this meant he was worried or not worried.

Hell again and then air conditioning, inside a little market with bright lights and an old man, bearded like a troll, who was already frowning.

Robin had the printed directions in her hand, and looked at them to read the name of the inn. "Excuse me?" she said. "We're lost? I think."

"Tourists from the road?" he said hoarsely.

"We're staying up the road, at the Little Swan?" Robin said. "We've just been antiquing around but now we got turned around."

The man scratched his brown beard. "Furniture?" he said, with no accent Robin could hear. "Is that the word? In your car with the summer?"

"The Little Swan?" Robin said again. She picked up a chocolate bar—was this how they acted, the locals, until you bought something, to make you feel stupid?—and looked outside at her husband smoking on the cement. The man whistled a long, low tone. "Always driving," he said. "Getting around it."

Robin looked around for the man's son or daughter, who left the ailing father in charge when things got slow. But now he was standing up. "You people," he said, firmly but without rancor. "Like the whole place is on fire, nitch." Nitch? *Bitch*, Robin thought, but could not feel better or worse. He limped toward her, or maybe the bright, checkered floor was uneven. He whistled again, and Robin looked out at her husband through the glass. Glenn got back into the car, waving at her impatiently, come on, come on, there's only one road.

"My husband and I—" Robin started, but the man had reached a shelf full of jars of nuts, and reached behind something to bring out a stick. A piece of wood, a log even, his arm fluttering with the weight of it. "Sunshine?" he said, as if repeating something Robin had said. She backed up. "Sunshine?"

Robin looked past even her husband to the hilly road, stretched away from this gas station she'd never see again once she got in the car and away from it. It had changed, was all: everything had changed somehow, tempted into a different way by some large, wrong thing. Glenn beckoned to her again, come on, and then waved the other way disgustedly, like to hell with you. Her wrong, wrong husband, his mean ways leaking all over the gravel and the dirt. Opposite the station was a field full of grass that curved along the road out of sight. And then what? And then where—where in the world? The vineyard? Two vineyards? The slanted fence? The restaurant, or the alley in back? That first shop with nothing? The shop she can't remember? Those birds desperate in the wind? Look at the vase, the flowerpot? The lobby of the inn, with the pamphlets of vineyards and scenery? Into the forest where the church waits to save the weary traveler? That field where someone was married long ago, with the wind whipping the veil and the words lost to the air, the guests leaning forward but still not catching a thing anyone said, like a ship in a bottle, lost to the ways of the wide, wide sea? Sunshine? Where could they go? What could they do? Drive forever, in a car that wasn't theirs, with each other or whoever that was, until late? It was getting late, wasn't it? Wasn't it? *They had to go somewhere.*

TAFI

an oral history recorded and edited by

ANNIE HOLMES AND PETER ORNER

These days, the rest of the world tends to see the Republic of Zimbabwe as an economic and human-rights catastrophe headed by a dictator, Robert Gabriel Mugabe, who brutalizes any opposition, seizes commercial farms, and won't let go the reins of power. Yet, not that long ago, upon the nation's independence from Britain in 1980, Zimbabwe, headed by Mugabe, was considered the hope of Southern Africa. In the 1980s, Zimbabwe seemed to have it all: a functioning democracy, a healthy economy and agricultural sector, and a reconciliation policy meant to mend years of bitter conflict between white settlers and black nationalists.

What went so wrong? A forthcoming collection of oral narratives, part of the Voice of Witness series, explores this complicated question through the life stories of diverse Zimbabweans—black, white, Indian; at home in Zimbabwe, and in exile in the ever-growing Zimbabwean diaspora.

We met Tafi in January 2009, at a safe house on the outskirts of Harare, the capital of Zimbabwe. Twenty-nine years old, friendly, outgoing, and athletic (in school, he excelled at the high jump), Tafi spoke calmly even as he described his imprisonment and torture. An activist in the Movement for Democratic Change, Tafi paid a severe price for organizing for the opposition. As we listened to his story, other torture survivors gathered around him on a long couch. Often they nodded in recognition.

I AM TAFI. I was born in Buhera in 1977, at the height of the liberation struggle. My village is just past the Buhera municipal offices on your way to Murambinda. When you reach the CHIVHU 80 KM peg or the Makombe Mission signpost, that's my area. It has about forty-eight households.

The headman of our village was a just man. He was a good headman because he was the former chief in our area, so he had much experience in dealing with local issues. And he also had an open heart to many different people. As kids we used to go to the circle that they call the *dare* in our culture, where trials take place. He was the kind of man who would do his duties without favor. He didn't care if the person in front of him was his relative. He was a man who just went for justice, no matter who it was. The issues he solved were mainly land disputes—someone getting into another person's boundary—and adultery, where one man would take the wife of another man. And whatever he decided, people listened to his judgment.

I am the fourth-born in a family of seven. I'm the youngest boy. After me come three girls. So I am the bridge from the boys to the girls. And since I was the last boy, I would do a lot of the girl work, you know, like the cooking, the fetching of firewood, the carrying of water from the neighboring wells, the laundry, the washing—I always did that with my sisters.

My father was the breadwinner; he was a mechanic. And he supported us. He sent us to school. His earnings did not give him enough to cover all our personal needs. We were struggling. He stayed in Harare and my mother would go and visit him. Because we were alone sometimes, my brothers and sisters and I are very close.

Usually after every two months, but sometimes longer—sometimes after three or four months—my father would finally come home to the rural areas. Those days when he came, I remember, were very merry, very jovial. Because after all that waiting, and after seeing other children whose fathers had come home and them always saying, "Look, my dad brought me this!" it was so nice for us to finally see him. He usually brought the family food and some clothes for us. There were also tennis balls for the children. And yes, I would feel proud that I had a caring father.

To supplement my father's income, my mother practiced the art of brewing traditional seven-days beer. First, she'd make some *sadza*.[1] Then she'd put it in a big container and leave that for two days to cool down, and she would put what we call *mumera*, the fermenting stuff, in the drum. Then it was left there until the fourth day. When it started fermenting—on the fifth day—she would burn it for the whole day, and then the next day she'd brew another recipe to mix in with it, and after that she'd filter the whole thing. Leave it for another day and night, the sixth day. The seventh day, that's the day for selling the beer. That morning my mother would wake up early and begin shouting with all her voice, like she had a loud speaker, "Beer today! Beer today! Beer today! Come with your blankets! The beer is very nice!" She would tell them to bring their blankets as a way of advertising. "Come with your blankets because when you become drunk you'll want to sleep."

We were a well-brought-up family. We were always helping my mother, fetching firewood, fetching water. We were always doing that. And she was proud of us, because we were obedient to her. And in a way we were like a point of reference to other young

[1] Stiff porridge, made from mealie (corn) meal.

children within our community. Their mothers would say, "Why don't you emulate what those boys and girls are doing? Look at them helping their mother, helping their family. You have to copy from them."

I would also do a lot of piece jobs. If a neighbor wanted his garden to be fenced, my brothers and I would do that in our spare time. We would sell some of our mangoes to supplement our family income. Also, of course, we took care of the cows, the goats, and the fowl.

But we had fun, too. My brothers and I spent a lot of time practicing martial arts, because in my rural area we were fortunate to have a man who was an expert in martial arts. We also sneaked off and swam in the Nyazvidzi River. We had to sneak because my mum discouraged us from swimming, because in our family we have an aunt who drowned in that water. My mum would say, "If you play in that river, the spirit of Auntie will call you and you will die in the water!" So we sneaked, but when we got home she would see that we'd been swimming, because our eyes would be red. And so she would beat us.

I've always been a good athlete. At school I did the triple jump. It goes *hop, step, jump*. Once I fractured my leg and spent two months in a cast. This discouraged me from continuing with the triple jump.

My favorite subjects in school were science, mathematics, and geography. I received high marks in those subjects. I was good in geography because I understand the environment. I've always been good at studying the weather. And from the oral stories we get from the old people within our community, I would know that if the weather is like this, the rains are about to come; if the pattern is like this, there will be some wind.

But our school was having problems. The way I understand it is that the school finances were being handled poorly, and one day the debt collectors came and took all the furniture. And so the next day when we went to school we had to sit on the floor because there were no chairs, no desks. And at this time we still had to pay school fees. There was no furniture and we were still made to pay 60¢ in school fees. At that time 60¢ was a big problem for a family with five children at school.

When I was older, I went to the mission school at Makombe. I went without my brothers. I was alone. And it was different from the kind of Christianity in my family, because the mission was Dutch Reformed Church. They have their own set of regulations.

I studied very hard. I had observed the learned people in my community, and I wanted to be one of them. Since we had no electricity, we used the firewood for light. There are some trees that will burn a flame like that of a candle, which can keep the room bright. So when we went into the forest to search for firewood, we would also search for those trees with a brighter light. And we used the fire to read, or we even read by the light of the moon.

But you know, some of your dreams don't come true. Because I was good at the sciences, I wanted to work in civil aviation. I wanted to work on airplanes. So at A-level I was working hard, doing mathematics, biology, and chemistry. But it was difficult. I failed. And when I failed, everything turned upside down. To go and study civil aviation, they wanted five points, and I had only two points. When I received my poor A-level results, I didn't know how I could go on. And money of course was a problem, too. So in '97, I left and came here to Harare.

In Harare, I was just like any other school-leaver looking for employment, but because it was the time of ESAP,[2] there were a lot

[2] Zimbabwe's IMF-imposed Economic Structural Adjustment Program. Intended to bring economic growth, it instead resulted in wide-scale unemployment.

of retrenchments[3] going on and so not a lot of work. My brother took me into his workshop and I worked as an assistant mechanic, but it was only for a while. He soon went broke, and since I didn't have any permanent accommodation to stay in town, I had to return to my rural area. It was then that I became involved in politics, spreading the word of the upcoming party, the MDC.[4] Morgan, its leader, comes from my area, and he is an inspiration to us. We thought, "Our son is from here. He's going to uplift the country collectively with us." And from 1999 to 2001, people were mostly not hostile to each other. Those who supported the MDC were not regarded by others as enemies, because we were working in a friendly way. But suddenly, in 2002, things changed very much.

Okay, yes, it's true that in 2000, there were some skirmishes where MDC homesteads were set on fire. And in my own village we had an incident where about seven homesteads were set on fire. This was reported in the *Daily News*. But after the presidential election of 2002, things got so much worse.

Arson became a big problem. ZANU-PF[5] supporters began burning the houses of MDC supporters. During that time the wife of Mr. Morgan Tsvangirai, then the Prime Minister designate, came to the area to sympathize with those people who had lost property. She brought blankets, food, and a little money. The affected people told the First Lady their stories. And that didn't go well with the ZANU guys. Especially in our village. There was one man, a war veteran who was the registrar of Buhera District at that time, who

---

[3] Layoffs.

[4] The Movement for Democratic Change.

[5] Zimbabwean African National Union–Patriotic Front. ZANU-PF is the ruling party in Zimbabwe, headed by President Robert Mugabe.

was discouraging us from supporting Morgan. He carried on a campaign, ordering the black boots[6] to come to our home area. He collaborated with the CIOs[7] and there was terror in Buhera.

Unfortunately, at this time my name was handed over to the Buhera police station. I and eleven other guys active in our area were informed that they were hunting us, that a riot of men were hunting us. Because there were false allegations that we eleven were the ones who were perpetrating all the arson. So we went and hid in the forest outside our village. It's relatively safe there. From the forest you can see the village. We spent two days sneaking around, and then some of my colleagues were caught. I myself tried to get out of Buhera by crossing the Nyazvidzi River. But I was unfortunate. I met the riot guys. One of the riot guys had seen a T-shirt on the drying line at my home. Now he saw that I was wearing that T-shirt. So he said "Ah! We see this T-shirt. Are you Tafi?" Because I also have dreadlocks, they knew it was me. And that was it.

I was then taken to Buhera Police Station. Some of the police there knew me. But no local police officers did the interrogation. They were police from Rusape, Mutare, Nyazura. And we heard that others had come from Harare, and there were also some Ndebele people.

When they torture you they call you one by one. You know, I was twenty-three years old then. When I first got taken in I was thinking that with police I was now safe. But later I realized that here, in this country, you are only safe when you are outside.

When they arrested me I was strong. I was fit, fit, fit, fit. And when I would get into trouble I always had my knuckles. But this was different. They said, "Strip off your clothes." And I removed my

---

[6] Popular term for overzealous officers from the police-support unit

[7] Officers of the CIO, the Central Intelligence Organization.

clothes. And then they beat me very, very thoroughly. And I remembering thinking, "Is this a war? The MDC has lost the presidential election, the election is over, now there is this violence?"

After they beat me they made me sit whilst naked. Then another officer came and said "Put your legs on the table." Then they brought a brick and told me to put my legs on top of the brick. Then they started beating my legs. They said they would beat me till I didn't produce any sound. They didn't tie my mouth, but they said, "The whip is going to tie your mouth until you produce no sound." I first complied. But the pain! I had to make sounds. And making some sounds was an irritation to the torturers. Then they would come and beat me more. I was beaten by *sjambok*, by baton stick, by manmade whips—small whips made with electrical wires. It was gruesome. I was told later they had to put icing sugar on my tongue because I lost consciousness.

During that time a politician came to the station to see us. A local ZANU-PF heavyweight. One by one we were brought to her, and she said to us, "You are the people who are causing problems here, who want democracy. Where was democracy when we were fighting the war of liberation?"

When I was called, for some reason she was given the wrong impression. She was thinking that she was going to find a gigantic man, a tall man. And so she said to the police, "Ahh. These little kids are troubling you? Why can't you just kill them?"

I remember something else also. One guy with us was called Paul, and when Paul was called they said, "Are you the Paul from the Bible? Now you have to die the second death."

We were denied food at Buhera Police Station. Our family members who would bring food were made to leave with the food, because we were considered as bandits or as terrorists within our own area. It was only after the lawyer came that we were given food. The

MDC sent him. This lawyer was later set on fire and chased away. He had to sneak out of Zimbabwe.

Then we were sent to Remand Prison in Rusape. There I experienced another way of torture. I was put in a coffin. They didn't kill me then, but it disturbed me very much because being in that coffin I could not help imagining being dead. Another way of torturing. When they released me from inside there, they hurried me up and said, "Stand on your own!" And from that darkness and from that confusion, automatically I fell right down.

In prison of course we lived with other inmates, non-political prisoners. When I first went into my cell those guys asked me to introduce myself. When I said my issue was political, I'm an MDC guy, those guys clapped their hands and said, "Yeah—you are doing some good. You are quite different from those who are here for stealing goats." So the inmates really liked us. But the prison officers didn't. They would come to us with pieces of newspaper, saying, "Country guys"—now they were calling us the country guys because they said we came from the rural areas to make trouble—"Country guys, have you seen this heading? 'The country guys were causing so many problems in Buhera.' But now look, where can you go? Have you looked around at these walls?"

When I was released, one of the conditions of the bail was that I couldn't return home to Buhera. I ended up going to the human-rights lawyers, who directed me to this safe house. Here, I was helped with medications. At that time I was worried about my body. I had been having bloody urine for quite some time. I don't know if it was from the beatings or whether I had developed some other problem. I also asked the doctor to examine my hand because I was having a lot of pain whenever I touched cold things. I later realized it was fractured.

It took me some time to recover. But right now I am feeling relatively stable. I am within average health, I would say. I have begun to understand and appreciate myself, and acknowledge those violations done to me. Some people died from those kinds of violations, so if you are still alive you have to thank God. I have also developed the art of self-realization, and the ability to let go of things, to not hold things on myself. If I hurt, I hurt. But then I release these feelings out of me.

Over the years we have had disappointments, politically, but like any other democrat I was expecting a change, hoping for it, and in March 2008 I was expecting that the long-awaited time of change had finally come. I worked on the campaign. I was involved in information-gathering and making a newsletter and distributing it to locations, rural areas. MDC was ready to win. They did win. And I was expecting that those people who perpetrated violence against innocent people would be tried in some way. Or if not tried, let them be accountable for the losses they brought upon us. Let the truth come out in the open. But all that changed after the 29th of March.

Instead of announcing MDC the winner, ZANU-PF delayed the release of the election results.[8] We published a newsletter that listed the actual figures from the polling stations. And the junta was not happy about that, because they were trying to suppress all other voices, and the truth, so we heard then that some of our MDC crews were kidnapped and murdered. At that time it was no longer safe for me. I was advised to get out of Zimbabwe, to go to Botswana, or even America. But I had a feeling, "I can't move out of Zimbabwe." Fortunately the human-rights lawyers were again able to secure a safe house for me. And this is the place.

Right now I am trying to not be involved in politics. I am trying

---

[8] ZANU-PF declared that the race had been too close, and that there was no outright winner. Due to election violence preceeding the runoff, MDC president Morgan Tsvangirai then dropped out of the race, and Mugabe maintained the presidency.

to help others heal by working as a counselor here at the safe house. My job is to listen to people, to help them tell their stories. And you know this healing work, you have to be very present, you know what I mean? You have to be humble, you have to be fair. You must try not to prejudge. You have to have empathy and try to understand other people's problems. It's so different from politics. In politics sometimes you have to show off. You want people to know who you are. And you do a lot of lying. There are times when you have to lie in order to escape from the police, the CIO, the army, because the actual truth can land you in prison. It's very different from the healing thing. I'm also doing some art now. But I'm still learning. My art is relatively poor! I'm trying painting, abstract painting. I also do art in the garden, growing herbs and vegetables. I'm also helping the others design a garden in the form of a labyrinth.

CONTRIBUTORS

MONA AWAD's fiction has appeared in *Matrix*, and received the Matrix/SLS Editors' Choice Award for Fiction in 2009. Her articles have appeared in the *Walrus*, the *Utne Reader*, and *Maisonneuve*, among other publications. She is currently pursuing an MScR in English Literature at the University of Edinburgh.

TOM BARBASH is the author of the novel *The Last Good Chance* and the nonfiction book *On Top of the World*. His short stories have appeared in *Tin House*, *One Story*, the *Virginia Quarterly Review*, *Narrative*, *Story*, *StoryQuarterly*, and elsewhere. He is an associate professor at California College of the Arts.

ARTHUR BRADFORD has published one book, *Dogwalker*, and is an O. Henry Award–winning short story writer. He created and directed the documentary series *How's Your News?*, which was broadcast on HBO, PBS, and, most recently, for one season on MTV.

TIM CARVELL is a writer for *The Daily Show with John Stewart*.

T. CORAGHESSAN BOYLE's most recent books are *The Women* and *Wild Child*. "The Wreck of the Beverly B." is excerpted from his next novel, *When the Killing's Done*, to be published by Viking in early 2011.

ERIC CALDERWOOD's essays have appeared in the *Virginia Quarterly Review*, the *American Scholar*, the *Boston Globe*, and elsewhere. He is a PhD student at Harvard, where his research focuses on Spain and Morocco.

SEAN CASEY lives in western Massachusetts. He runs The Chuckwagon, a chapbook press. He is a recent graduate of the MFA Program for Poets and Writers at the University of Massachusetts. A story of his is forthcoming in *Columbia: A Journal*.

JULIO VILLANUEVA CHANG is the founding editor of *Etiqueta Negra*, and the author of *Elogios Criminales*, a book of profiles. He is the winner of the Interamerican Press Association Award in feature writing, and his nonfiction has appeared in the *Virginia Quarterly Review* and The *Believer*.

BRIDGET CLERKIN was born and raised in Southern California and now lives in Manhattan. "Twenty Questions" is her first published story.

LAWRENCE-MINH BÙI DAVIS's work has appeared in the *New York Quarterly*, the *Louisville Review*, *AGNI Online*, and *Fiction International*. He is co-editor of the *Asian American Literary Review*. "Like the Locked Antlers" is an excerpt from a novel in progress.

ANTHONY DOERR is the author of *The Shell Collector*, *About Grace*, and *Four Seasons in Rome*. His fourth book, a collection of stories titled *Memory Wall*, will be published by Scribner in July.

BRIAN T. EDWARDS teaches literature at Northwestern. He is the author of *Morocco Bound*, and has published essays in the *Believer*, *Public Culture*, *Foreign Policy*, and other publications. He edited a special section on new Egyptian writing for the ninth issue of *A Public Space*.

DANIEL HANDLER is the author of three novels. His new book as Lemony Snicket, a collaboration with Maira Kalman entitled *13 Words*, will be published this fall.

JOHN HODGMAN's most recent book is *More Information Than You Require.*

ANNIE HOLMES, a Zimbabwean filmmaker and writer, directs communications for an international feminist network and has published a short memoir, *Good Red*, and various short stories. An associate editor on *Underground America: Narratives of Undocumented Lives*, she is working with Peter Orner on a collection of first-person narratives of Zimbabweans for the McSweeney's Voice of Witness series.

JULIE KLAUSNER is a comedy writer and performer whose first book, *I Don't Care About Your Band*, was released earlier this year. Her website, predictably, is julieklausner.com.

SODIENYE KURUBO lives in Port Harcourt, Nigeria, and recently qualified to practice as a lawyer. He has never been to the U.S., legally or illegally.

DAVID MEANS was born and raised in Michigan. His second collection of stories, *Assorted Fire Events*, won the Los Angeles Times Book Prize for Fiction, and was a finalist for the National Book Critics Circle Award. His third, *The Secret Goldfish*, was shortlisted for the Frank O'Connor International Short Story Prize. His fourth, *The Spot*, will be published next month by Faber and Faber.

PETER ORNER, editor of *Underground America*, is the author of the novel *The Second Coming of Mavala Shikongo*, a finalist for the *Los Angeles Times* Book Prize, and *Esther Stories*, a *New York Times* Notable Book and finalist for the Pen/Hemingway Award. He lives in San Francisco.

DAVID SHIELDS is the author of ten books, including, most recently, *Reality Hunger: A Manifesto*.

SARAH VOWELL's most recent book is *The Wordy Shipmates*.

(Above: Brian Evenson, novelist and McSweeney's subscriber)